THE DEVIL'S STOP

A JACK WIDOW THRILLER

SCOTT BLADE

Black Lion Media

ALSO BY SCOTT BLADE

1

THE MAN HAD FORGOTTEN his own name. But not because of some sort of traumatic brain injury like a car accident or a plane crash or falling off a ladder. It was nothing like that. It wasn't from a baseball bat to the head. Although that wasn't out of the question. Not yet. It wasn't from a gunshot to the brain, which was what he was hoping for.

The man wore a US Air Force flight suit. At least that's what it looked like to the others. That's what it looked like to anyone who didn't know any better. The suit's fabric was all green. Standard issue for the men in his crew, in his line of work, which is a small, elite group of airmen.

This man was in that group. He was an airman. The uniform he wore was standard-issue for most of the airmen in crews like his, and there were lots of crews like his.

The uniform he had been issued was all green, but the one he wore now wasn't all green anymore. When he had left for work the day before to work a twenty-four-hour shift, it had been. It had been pristinely washed and ironed and ready for a workday's wear and tear.

That may not seem like a lot, but for a guy in his profession, it was. It was a lot because he didn't work a nine-to-five shift like the rest of the professional world. He worked twenty-four and forty-eight-hour shifts, and sometimes even seventy-two hours. It all depended. It was all relative.

Like his coworkers, he often had to sleep at work in split shifts. Usually, there was one man awake and one man asleep. And then sometimes there were both men awake at the same time.

This was how it went. Work, sleep, repeat.

The longest shift he'd ever worked was five days. But that was only once. And not at this installation. That was back in North Dakota.

The shift he'd just gotten off, early that afternoon, was a forty-eight-hour one. And the next shift was also forty-eight hours, which he had told his captors. He had told them when the next shift ends. They had needed to know that. He was sure he told them, pretty sure. He must have, because they weren't asking him about it. Not anymore.

His uniform had been in the same pristine condition when he left work, before he got here, in this situation. But now, it wasn't.

Now, his Air Force uniform was no longer pristine, no longer clean, and there was not much green left visible, not anywhere on it. Now, the uniform was a mixture of blood reds and dried blood blacks.

The man's name patch was no longer legible. The letters on the patch, like most of his uniform, were pasted over with an outside substance.

It was blood.

It was his blood.

The man was having problems remembering his own name, but he knew his own blood.

Blood is the kind of thing that is self-evident.

It was splattered across his name patch and uniform. It was splattered all over his chest and neck and face. It was probably all over his pants, too, but he couldn't be sure. He was having problems craning his head forward so that he could see his legs.

His legs were no longer mobile, so he couldn't raise them into view either. They had been beaten and smashed so severely that they were paralyzed or broken, or both. It wasn't clear to him. Either way, he could no longer feel them or move them.

A hazy, black, smoky odor filled his nostrils, along with a discernible smell of over-barbequed meat. The smells were carried by the hard wind. It was impossible for him not to notice. It was pungent and bitter and harsh.

One of his captors stood close to him and repeated the same question he'd asked before. He remembered that much. It hit him like déjà vu. He remembered answering before and in detail. He remembered giving latitude and longitude. He remembered giving landmarks, which weren't many, a mountain to the north, another to the south, a lake twenty-two miles in one direction, a little house on the corner of the next road over, but that was it. There were no main roads anywhere in sight. There was only one way in and one way out, besides helicopter access.

"Where is it?" one of his captors asked him.

Like before, the airman repeated the same answer, giving up coordinates and a road name and a description of the little house nearby. But, like before, he reminded them they'd never get past the armed security, and even if they did, they'd never get past all the computerized checks, nor would they be able to do any of it without an airman of his qualifications.

The captor ignored his warnings, also like before.

The airman went back to his previous desire. He wanted to die. He wanted it so badly that he would've told them anything they asked if he knew the answer. And if he didn't, then he'd lie about it.

He prayed for a quick death. The faster, the better. The sooner, the better.

He wanted death, unlike anything that he had ever wanted before in his life. He wanted it more than breath. He wanted it more than freedom.

Death superseded everything else. It superseded his training and his life.

The man was technically from the 320th Air Expeditionary Wing. He used to be anyway, before this new assignment. The 320th Air Expeditionary Wing's motto was Strength through Awareness.

He was an airman.

The airman had lost his strength two hours and thirty minutes ago. He only knew that because he had been counting the seconds in his head. The only thing you could do to distract yourself from immense pain and torture was to recite something in your head, something memorized, something unforgettable. That's how they had taught him to do it. Only they had taught him to recite the Pledge of Allegiance. He couldn't do that anymore—not today. Instead, he switched to counting. Hard to forget the number system. It was easier to forget his own name.

As for the rest of his unit's motto, he had no awareness left. That left him right after his strength.

His natural survival instinct gave up on him hours earlier.

They trained you for this, he told himself.

Remember your training. He repeated, over and over. But it was useless. His training had abandoned him, too.

He wanted them to kill him. He pleaded for mercy, not for his life, not to be spared, but for a quick death, an end to it.

Kill me! Please! he thought he had said, but he didn't.

He'd said nothing. Not for a while now. He had gone limp a few times. Maybe he had blacked out. He couldn't remember. Perhaps he had blacked out, and they had woken him up.

He thought about a bullet to the head, or to the heart, or anywhere to make it all stop, and stop now. It became the only thing that mattered to him. It became the only thought in his brain.

There was almost nothing he wouldn't tell them or do to get a single merciful bullet. There wasn't any question he wouldn't answer at this point.

He remembered he was supposed to say his name and rank.

Did he say that? He couldn't remember. His head hurt.

He had top security clearance of the highest order that a man of his rank and station could get. He remembered that. He had to have top security clearance. It was critical to his job description. Your crew needs top security clearance when they have a direct line from the president. And his crew had direct access both to and from the president of the United States, himself. Not a staffer. Not an underling. Not a cabinet member. Not even to the vice president. The access was simple, direct, and clearly marked—no interference between the president and his crew. Day or night, the president could contact him.

Full stop.

But his captors hadn't asked him about that. They hadn't seemed the least bit interested in his security clearance or his access or the reasons he had direct access. They weren't interested because they already knew.

He had already told them.

The pain he felt was so unbearable that if they had asked him, he would've given up his presidential access, easy.

Anything for that bullet.

Midnight darkness loomed everywhere, all around them, around the vast forest, surrounding the nine men outside the wood cabin. Violent rain beat down for miles in every direction. It poured and slammed down on the cabin's high, shingled roof, and the ground outside, and through the trees. The rain thumped into the trees like loose bullets falling from the sky. Mud loosened and flowed in long, uneven streams down the footpath back to a parked F-150, engine off, headlights on, coning out into vivid beams of wet light.

The rain clattered and crashed and slammed into the trees and terrain so hard, and his head hurt so badly that he couldn't recall a time when the earth wasn't covered in torrential rainfall.

The only thing louder than the rain was the cold, merciless wind. The wind stormed and yowled through the trees like a nuclear siren.

Nuclear sirens. He knew something about that. They all did, his whole crew. It was their nightmare scenario. The only thing worse than the screeching of nuclear sirens was that direct line to the president ringing. It was the nightmare of his entire crew. It was what they were trained for, but it was what they dreaded the most. They had the only job in the world like that. Their jobs required cold, calculated actions, precise actions. They were trained to endure the worst-case scenarios. They were trained to eat a bullet before they gave in to terrorists, to the enemy.

They were the last line of defense. Their jobs made them the most revered, and the most feared men on the planet.

And he was sure he had betrayed all of that by giving in, by giving up information that he wasn't supposed to give up.

Lightning strikes cracked infrequently, far in the distance, on the horizon, lighting up the sky, the tops of the immense trees, and the shadowing mountains, which loomed massive and mammoth, like the tombs of giants.

No thunder. Not anywhere. Not that any of them could hear. There was only the rain, the wind, and the sparse lightning cracks, and then there were the fires.

The things in the fires were the only things that mattered to him other than his own life. At that moment, all he cared about was the things in the fires and quick death. The things in the fires mattered to him because they had been more than his friends. They had been his crew, his guys. They had been under him in rank.

This was all his fault.

His wrists were nailed to the hard, wet timber on the porch's wall. He hung, crucified by nails fired out of a nail gun.

He had once been a Marine, a tough breed, long before he transferred to the USAF.

He was proud of his Marine Corps years. He always thought that had made him tougher than his counterparts. But no one would know that now, not if they looked at his face. His face was bludgeoned and bloody. His one good eye was utterly void of all hope. Nothing about it registered as a former Marine.

His right eye was bashed and battered closed. He'd never see out of it again. The iris was cracked and splintered to the point of grayness, to where it would have to be enucleated, not amputated, like an arm or a leg, but enucleated. The internal nerves were dislocated and ripped. If he had ever opened that eye again, it'd have no color left.

If he ever opened it again, but he wouldn't.

He stared down with his left eye at four severed fingers, and one severed thumb plopped down on the porch's planks. Rain and blood pooled together between the removed digits, making them look like pieces of meat covered in cooking oil, waiting to be fried, like sausage links.

The fingers and thumb had been cut off using a pair of butcher shears; the kind used to cut through animal bone and pretty much anything else placed between the curved blades.

He stared down at the lost extremities. He knew they were his, but he felt nothing. No panic. No sense of saving them. No desire to even think about it. Nothing.

He would never have them again. No one was going to reattach them. He knew that for sure.

He knew that because his captors had seared his new stumps with a hot poker that they had pulled out of a wood-burning stove in the cabin's modest kitchen.

Several feet away from his fingers, he saw some of his broken teeth. He saw two incisors and three molars. They were scattered in the mud. The man who had done this to him had jerked them out with pliers and tossed them like salt over his shoulder.

The airman had lost count of how many teeth he had left. He knew there were some because they had scraped his tongue as he licked his lips and coughed. He spat blood that was from a stream of blood, running down his face from a viciously broken nose.

They had broken it with a good old-fashioned knuckleduster.

All the horror that he had experienced that night, personally, wasn't the worst of it. The worst of it had been watching his two crewmen getting the same and then getting far worse.

He craned his head one last time and looked over to the right. Right there, out in a small clearing in front of the cabin, he saw them, the things in the fires. He had watched the last one die. He had heard the last one scream for the last time, until the screams became part of the screeching winds.

Now, all he saw were two separate, raging fires. One fire still moved. The thing in the fire still twitched involuntarily.

The airman said, "Mitch?"

He had watched his crew members, his friends, burn alive. Then he saw the man with the blowtorch step back into view. The sight of him was worse than a nightmare. It was worse than a monster under the bed because it was real.

The airman spat out blood again. This time splinters of one of his remaining teeth came out with it.

Barely audible, he spoke, taking deep, quick gasps of air in between words.

"No! Wait! I told you. I told you where it is. The coordinates are right. I gave you what you wanted. What else do you want?"

A second man stepped behind the man with the blowtorch. He was taller than the one with the blowtorch. His face was long, horse-like. Two wicked H-shaped scars gashed across his temple like tick marks on a chalkboard. Two parts of his eyebrow were missing where hair didn't grow anymore. He had a big, thick beard like the others. His eyes were deep-set and brown, but far closer to black than brown.

The man was pale white, like a ghost. So was the blowtorch-man. His skin was also pale. The rest of them were all dark tan, like cowboys who worked out in the sun all day, but under the clothes, they were equally pale.

The man with the H-shaped scars was obviously the leader. He was the one giving the orders. He was the one asking the questions. He was the one who spoke. He was the first man the airman saw when they ambushed him.

At first, he'd wondered if it was because he wore his uniform out in public. If that was how they identified him? He wasn't supposed to wear his greens in public. That's why he had been ordered to keep them in his locker, but he hadn't listened. He had driven back to the house wearing them.

It turned out not to be the reason he had been identified, because his crew members were already captured. They were already shoved into the bed of the pickup truck, hands and feet and mouths already duct-taped.

The airman didn't know how they had been identified or captured or ambushed. He guessed it was as easy as anything. Most ambushes are easy because of the element of surprise. That, and trust. He had walked into the house he shared with the other two crew members and trusted that it was all good, that it was all normal. It wasn't.

He had walked into a trap. Why wouldn't he? Who would think that armed mercenaries were waiting for him inside his home?

The man with the H-shaped scars was the highest-ranking man there. Concerning military units, he was Major. That was how the airman thought of it.

Major grabbed the arm of the man with the blowtorch and pulled him back, like he was wrangling a wild animal, a vicious pet, like an attack dog. Which he was.

Major stepped forward, and Attack Dog stepped back. The rain picked up its pace and pounded harder around them, as if it was growing angry. The raindrops were on the verge of becoming hard hail.

The airman had his only remaining ear tuned in and heard rushing streams of rainwater and crackling of flames from the things in the fires. He wondered how long before his friends would be put out by the rain? However long it took didn't matter, anyway. Their bodies were already burned beyond recognition. The only thing that would remain of them would be ashy human forms, like the remains of vampires who were captured by villagers and executed by bursting into flames under the midday sunlight.

The thought was ghastly, yet he couldn't let it go. He didn't want to let it go because if he stopped focusing on his dead men, then the thought that came back to him was the thought of death.

A tear rolled down from the remaining eye of the airman.

Major saw this and stepped closer, close enough for the airman to smell his breath. He recognized the smell immediately. It was a variety of things, but whiskey was the main ingredient.

Major knew the airman smelled his breath. He breathed out, exhaling the whiskey fumes toward the man's broken nose.

"You like that smell?"

The airman said nothing.

Major reached out and violently grabbed a tuft of airman's hair. He jerked the airman's head back and slammed it into the cabin's outer wall. With his other hand, Major lifted an object, slim and sleek and wet from the rain. It was black and terrifying. It looked like a short-barreled modified shotgun, only smaller and a little more terrifying because the airman knew what it was.

The gun had a colossal magazine stuffed into the base. The gun was the nail gun. It was the most violent nail gun he had ever seen, and he had seen a lot of carpentry tools. Like a lot of men from New England, he had grown up in a house where instead of a garage, his dad had put together a colossal tool shed.

"No! No!" he begged.

Major brought the barrel of the nail gun close to the airman's face; pausing it, leaving it, drawing it and pulling it back to give a sense of relief and then bringing it back to his face, slowly. He repeated this like a cannibal who was playing with his food.

Major was a sadistic man.

The nail gun's muzzle skimmed the chin of the airman; then it slowly coasted over his lips, flicked his nose, and stopped dead over his good eye.

Major was a big guy, but not stocky, not like Attack Dog, but still massive. He was dressed like a biker. He wore a flannel shirt under a black leather vest covered in patches from a violent motorcycle club. The flannel shirt was unbuttoned at the top. The top three buttons flapped open, showing the top of his chest.

The airman stared down at Major's neck. Major wanted him to look. He wanted him to see what dangled there.

Major wore dog tags around his neck. Several of them. Most of them were shined clean, but two pairs of them were smeared with wet blood. They were fresh. They had belonged to the friends of the airman, to the things in the fire. Before Major lit them ablaze, he'd stripped them of their dog tags and put them on, like trophies from a fresh kill.

Major reached up with his free hand and scooped up the dog tags that were wrapped around the neck of the airman. Slowly, he pulled them upward, choking the airman; then he jerked down hard, and the tags came off.

Major lifted them, letting them dangle in front of the eye of the airman, next to the nail gun. Then he lowered them and shoved them into his pocket, out of sight.

Major stared at him with his cold, black eyes. Then he moved the nail gun aside, just an inch, to the bridge of the nose of the airman. But he slanted it up a degree as if to suggest that he was aiming the next nail to fire right into a targeted region of the brain of the airman. Which he was.

Major made sure that the airman saw it.

"Where is it?"

"I told you. I gave you the location."

Major paused a long beat.

"You're sure that you're giving me the right coordinates?"

The airman coughed up more blood.

"Yes! Kill me! Please!"

Major let the answer hang out there in the air like he was letting the airman mull it over, reconsider it.

"What about the next crew?"

"What?"

"The graveyard crew? Do they know?"

"Know what?"

"Do they know about us? Did you sound the alarm?"

The working eye of the airman flicked back and forth, pointing east, pointing west, desperate like the cavalry was coming to save him at any moment.

No one came.

"What alarm?"

Foolish.

Major whipped the nail gun up and over the man's head and to the side and fired it.

A nail exploded out of the barrel and hit the wood behind his head. The nail, the wood, the explosion from the barrel, had all been so close to the man's head that it would've deafened his ear on that side of his head if it had still been there. But it wasn't.

Ear or no ear, the airman still felt the violent vibration in the back of his skull. It reverberated through his head like a marble in a can.

He closed his good eye tight, expecting to be shot, hoping to be dead, praying that he would be dead. But he wasn't.

He opened his eye.

"Please. They know nothing. I didn't warn anyone."

Major looked at him for another long moment.

"Kill me! Please!" he begged again.

Major's eyes opened wide and slow and then narrowed. He understood. The airman wanted death. He yearned for a quick release, for an escape.

Major released the man's tuft of hair and stepped back. He called out to Attack Dog, who stepped forward, gladly, obediently. Major handed the nail gun back, and Attack Dog took it like it was the only thing in life that mattered to him. But Major didn't give up his weapon to be unarmed. He kept his now empty hand out and said, "Blowtorch."

Attack Dog smiled and handed the blowtorch to him.

Four other men in heavy rain slickers, hooded, all big and tall and loyal guys, like a pack of wild dogs, stood around in a wide formation that looked trained, almost like an elite military unit, like they had been together, trained together, and gone out on missions together in a past life.

The airman screamed and shouted, "NO! NO! NO!"

Major said, "Shout all you want. No one can help you now, but you."

Major stepped back close and showed the airman the tip of the flame from the blowtorch. It burned blue.

"You're a strong guy. I've never seen a man endure what you have endured here today. I torture you. Your friends. I burn them alive, and yet you stay strong."

"No! I'm not strong! Kill me!"

Major smiled and laughed, an evil laugh as if he enjoyed this, like a madman waking to find the door to his cell wide open.

"You're right. You're not the strongest I've tortured. Not even close."

"I'm not! Kill me!"

"I'll kill you, eventually. After you tell me what I want to know."

"I know nothing else! I told you everything!"

Major pursed his lips and made a sound while shaking his head slowly, taunting the airman like a schoolyard bully.

"Do you have children?"

The face of the airman froze like he was thinking about the question. Major noticed.

"No."

Major nodded and said, "Too bad, because your seed will die with you. I'm going to burn your testicles off now."

The airman said nothing, but his eye began darting from side to side again.

"I hear that to be very painful. Even though the torch burns too hot for you to feel anything. It's all mental, you see."

"No! Please! I told you everything!"

"Do they know?"

"No one knows."

"Did you trip an alarm? Have you signaled to them?"

"No! I swear!"

Major reached into his pocket with his free hand and pulled out a crumpled slip of white paper. He uncrumpled it and stared at it, then he flipped it around and showed it to the airman.

"We go to these coordinates. We go down there to get what we want. Are we gonna find the business end of an AIM-9 Sidewinder?"

The man just stared at him, fear in his eyes.

"Did you warn anyone?"

"No! No! How could I?"

Major looked into the man's good eye for a long moment. Eventually, he retreated and crumpled the paper back up and shoved it into his pocket.

He reached up and patted the man's head tauntingly.

"Okay. Okay. I believe you."

Major handed the blowtorch back to Attack Dog.

"Kill me now! Please!"

Major backed away and stopped and spoke.

"Just one more question. Where's the other one?"

"What?"

"There're supposed to be four of you."

"No! There's not! Just three!"

"Where's the other one?"

"There's not!"

Major frowned.

"This time, I don't believe you."

"It's true! I don't know where he is!"

Major looked at him.

The airman had given it away. They both knew it.

"You don't know where he is?"

The airman said nothing. He was feeling scrambled, confused. Had there been four of them? Had there been another member of his crew?

He couldn't remember.

Major smiled and said, "I believe you."

He reached into a vest pocket, slowly, and pulled out a cigar that he had been smoking for a few days. He liked to take puffs when he was in the mood, and now he was in that mood. He pulled out an expensive gold Zippo. He flipped the lighter to light, and he put the cigar in his mouth, brought the flame to the cigar's foot, and lit it.

He puffed away, blowing the smoke into the man's face.

Major returned the Zippo to the pocket of his jeans and continued to enjoy the cigar.

Attack Dog stood by, ready.

"Please! Kill me!" the man begged again.

Major ignored him again, and stared out into the rain and then back down at the burning bodies.

He called out to Attack Dog.

"Yes?"

"Gas him up."

The airman heard the order but didn't understand at first. Not until he saw Attack Dog's eyes. Not until he watched Attack Dog coming at him with one thing on his mind.

That's when he knew. Attack Dog set down the blowtorch and picked up a half-empty gas can, metal and red like a fire truck.

The man called out.

"NO! NO!"

It was pointless.

His heart raced as the contents of the gas-can emptied over him, uncaringly. Gasoline splashed everywhere. It poured down and burned his good eye. It burned his nose. Some of it got into his mouth, and he swallowed it. The liquid fumed and nearly choked him.

Attack Dog shook the can at the end to make sure he'd used every drop.

The airman never stopped begging, but his voice stopped working. It ran dry. They no longer heard his pleas. It would have made no difference, but he tried anyway.

Attack Dog tossed the empty gas can out into the darkness and picked up the blowtorch again.

"No," Major ordered. "Switch that off."

Attack Dog didn't argue. He followed orders. He switched off the torch.

Major beckoned to Attack Dog and gave them all an order.

"Saddle up, boys. Let's head out."

Attack Dog nodded and stepped off the porch into the rain. His long hair was drenched in the rain. The rain beat down on his face, battering his eyes, but he didn't flinch. His eyes stayed open.

The four men standing in formation broke and walked down the path to the F-150.

Attack Dog followed them.

The airman watched.

Major stayed where he was. He stepped off the porch, rain covering him. He stood by the burning corpses and smoked the rest of his cigar. Then he looked at the airman.

He said, "This country has gone to hell."

The man said nothing.

"It's gone to hell, and no one does a thing about it. No one cares. They're all blind to it."

The airman hung by his wrists and continued to listen.

"The politicians in Washington. The bastards in the White House. The assholes in Congress. The justices in the court. The cops on the street. The soldiers out there fighting. Even the citizens in their beds. They don't know. But we're going to change that. I want you to know that. I want you to know. We're going to reboot everything. All of it."

Sheer, unadulterated terror came over the remains of the airman's face. He thought of someone close to him. And he was unequivocally afraid of what Major was going to do with what he had taken possession of. He hoped they would never learn how to operate it.

Silence fell over them for a long minute, and Major finished the cigar. With the last bit of it in his mouth, he stood straight and saluted the airman.

Then he stepped back and took the cigar out of his mouth and aimed it.

Before he tossed it, he said, "Thank you for your service, Captain."

He threw the cigar at the airman's feet. It hit the porch. The gasoline lit up in a fast WHOOSH!

Major turned and walked down the footpath.

The airman screamed.

Major joined his guys down by the F-150. Attack Dog got into the truck with one other guy, and Major and the other three men got onto their wet motorcycles, put on their helmets, and revved the engines.

Seconds later, they pulled off down a rugged dirt trail and drove away.

The airman's screams were swallowed by the flames and the rain until the cabin went up in the fire.

Fighting to grow, the fires burned against the hard rain.

2

At dawn, Jack Widow made a life-threatening decision. Only he didn't know it. It was a wrong choice, the kind of wrong choice that anyone might've made. It was all by chance. Anyone could see that it was the wrong choice afterward, in the post-game analysis.

If there were after-action reports of things to come his way, this would be the decision that turned everything wrong. He would've been blamed for the deadly outcome that would plow straight through his life in the days to come.

At six-foot-four, Widow stood solemn and alone and statuesque and weathered, all like an outmoded old water tower. He looked like a giant lost on the side of the road to the motorists on the highway.

He was unaware of the deadly mistake he was about to make. Widow also was completely unaware that he stood twenty-five miles away from where a cabin had burned the night before.

Widow turned his head, shifting it due south, stopping southeast, toward a guesstimation of the direction of the state of his birth, Mississippi.

He stared in that direction for a long moment. He let his mind wander back to a different realm, a different life, his first life. If there was a god in the afterlife keeping score, tallying up all the lives a man lived, then technically he was on his third, or maybe it was his fourth. It was hard for him to keep track since he was no longer in the business of lying to protect his cover.

Widow had grown up in a small town in Mississippi, the son of a sheriff mother and a drifter father. His mother raised him on her own, with her own money and with her own capabilities. She had done the best she could with the little she had. He had no complaints, not now.

But back then, he did—just one big one.

She had lied to him his whole childhood. She had lied about who his father had been. He still didn't know the man. Not now. Not ever.

She had told him that his father was some sort of army hero who died in combat. That turned out not to be true. She came clean when he was seventeen. Feeling betrayed, Widow ran away from home, joined the Navy. He stayed quiet for sixteen years, never speaking to his mother the whole time. Not once. No phone calls. No postcards. Not one word.

Not until the day some asshole shot her and left her for dead. She was left laid out in a ditch, bleeding and near death, and he wasn't there for her.

Widow came off an undercover assignment to return home— all of that to see her only one last time in a hospital bed, where she died.

Widow's second life had been in the Navy and NCIS after he ran away from home, where he became the best of the best. He worked undercover as a Navy SEAL, which meant that he had to be a SEAL. In order to keep his identity believable, he had to train, and go out on black-op missions with, the SEAL teams. He followed orders and rose through the ranks like an ordinary SEAL team member. He had killed like a standard SEAL.

It also meant that he had to avoid getting close to people. He had avoided friends. He had avoided love.

No one knew his real job except the NCIS.

No other way around it. It couldn't be faked.

No way could he impersonate a SEAL whenever he was needed to go out on assignment like one of those forty-five-minute TV dramas portrayed undercover cop life.

That kind of thing might've been how spies did it, or under-cover FBI agents or DEA or other secret groups.

Maybe those guys had agents who went undercover with a false identity for a limited time until the job was done.

Not Widow. Not his team.

Widow had to be the real deal. He had to be a SEAL. He had to go all the way.

If you counted his childhood, his early Navy life, his SEAL life, and now his life as a drifter, then he was on life number four, he guessed, and not three. But who was really counting?

Mississippi was way too far away to be seen from where he was. From where he stood, he might as well have been looking down from outer space, trying to find the state. The distance was too far away. His childhood was too long ago. He knew that. But even a stray dog thinks of home from time to time.

Yesterday, Widow had stopped in a place called New London, Connecticut, a coastal Navy town. Beautiful place. It felt like home, even though he had never been there before. It felt like home because there was an NCIS installation there. It was on the Naval base.

While he was there, the thought of visiting had crossed his mind. And he even came close around lunchtime, when he stopped in an off-base coffee shop, hoping to glimpse sailors coming in on their lunch breaks, in uniform. It was the same hope of someone revisiting his old alma mater.

It felt like home; only it wasn't. It was just a cozy memory that resurged through him because it was homelike.

He visited none of the Naval installations. No interest. He'd ended up there the same way that he'd ended up now on the side of the road, deep in the country in northern New Hampshire: life compelled him. That, and he had caught a bus and gotten off there.

Widow took one last look toward Mississippi, toward the past, and then he killed the thought and looked down at the road under his feet, and then at his surroundings.

He was standing at a crossroads, an uneven one. It was uneven because one road was an old highway that headed north into Canada. And the second was a forgotten road to God knows where in both directions.

He looked up in four different directions, like the four points of a broken compass—left, right, back, and front. Left was almost west. Right was practically east. Back was sort of south. And forward was close to straight-on north.

The points of this compass were not perfect, but close enough to be a little suspicious, as if they had been designed that way on purpose.

Some cheap architect right out of college, working for the state, probably did it as a gag or a little secret that only he knew about, the way artists paint themselves into the background of their paintings and never tell a soul.

In all four directions, for Widow, there was a choice to be made, a direction to be taken, a road to take.

Widow stood dead on a crossroads that he had never heard of, and he wondered, why not? In the world he loved, the Americana world, it would be famous, like Route 66. But it wasn't.

He had never heard of it before.

The crossroads was more of a cross than a traditional X. One road was an old, two-lane highway, reliably maintained but not glorified with new blacktop. It led out of sight in two directions, and the other wasn't quite a dirt track, but not far from it if the state didn't come along and repave it soon.

It looked like it had been created during the days of horse and buggy about two hundred years ago, maybe more, and in the time since, it was blacktopped maybe ten times, with the last time being well over a decade in the past.

The old track led off into two opposite, yet equally forested, equally mountainous, and equally rugged directions.

The highway backtracked a hundred-plus miles back down along the Vermont-New Hampshire border, and eventually became the end of Route Three and from there led down to Massachusetts, where Widow had spent two days with a girl who had talked with him, slept with him, shared coffee with him, but never told him a thing about her own private life.

This was all after he was in New London, and a lot more memorable.

The girl had a palpable need for privacy, which Widow respected. His life was an open book for anyone to read, but no one ever did. She asked no questions of him, other than the basics. And he asked no questions of her, other than the basics.

After two days fizzled out, he left her and headed north to continue a hollow quest that he had taken upon himself to go on, which entailed visiting all of what he called Devil Stops in the US.

Hell's Kitchen was the last stop he'd made. He'd gotten the idea when he was in Hells Canyon, back in Idaho. Then he moved on to Devils Lake in Wisconsin. After that, he headed east to Hell, Michigan, and then on to Route 666 in Pennsylvania, and to Hell's Kitchen, where he went a little off course and stopped in New London, out of curiosity.

All this until he was headed north to a place called Omen Bay in Maine. That had been the plan and the last stop on his invented itinerary until he accidentally sat in a bus terminal for ninety minutes before he realized it was decommissioned.

The depot looked in use. The service drive into it was unblocked, and the lights were on, but there were no workers, no other passengers waiting, and no buses came through. Eventually, he figured it out and felt stupid for not seeing it earlier.

It was at this abandoned bus depot, and out of boredom, that he looked over a bulletin board posted with government information packets and an old state map of New Hampshire's roads and highways.

On the map, he saw a town name that interested him.

The town was in the middle of nowhere. It was called Hellbent, New Hampshire.

Hellbent. It fit his current itinerary. It was maybe the best name for a Devil Stop yet. He had to check it out. Besides, he had nothing to lose. He wasn't on any real timeline. No schedule to keep.

He was a man with a regimented past who lived for an uncertain future, full of surprise.

That was the route he'd taken that led him to now. Standing at the crossroads that led in three directions he didn't want to go, and one he did, to Hellbent.

How he got there specifically was on a bus from a different terminal a mile away from the closed one. This bus dropped him off south about twenty miles, where he hitched rides until he caught a ride from two friendly Canadians headed back to their country. They were happy to drop him off where he now stood, just fifteen minutes earlier.

He had seen no other cars since.

The reason the crossroads were so interesting, other than leading to the town of Hellbent, were the words involved.

The names involved, to be more precise.

The highway that Widow stood on was the Daniel Webster Highway—named after a famous New Hampshire statesman and lawyer. The other road had no posted name that Widow could see, but there was a forgotten street sign off to the side that was posted. It read: This way to Hellbent.

Hellbent? Daniel Webster?

A crossroads of Daniel Webster Highway and a road that led to Hellbent?

The Devil and Daniel Webster.

He wondered how this had happened. What were the odds?

After another five minutes passed, Widow looked in all directions again. Still, there were no cars.

He looked at the map in his head and recalled a mountain range that he would like to look at.

He stepped away from the crossroads and stared over the trees, veering down into a grassy valley with treetops as thick as grenade bursts. The sun beamed to the east. Widow cupped his eyes, making a visor out of his hands. He couldn't see the mountains that way. Not surprising. In his mind, he calculated the distance from the crossroads to the particular mountain range he sought to be around eighty-five miles, give or take a mile.

The mountains that he looked for were called the Presidential Range. He was too far north to see them. He had never seen them before. In fact, he had only passed through New Hampshire by interstate or over it by air, never stopping. Never even giving it a second thought, which he realized was shameful.

New Hampshire was a historic American state, one of the original thirteen colonies. The first men who lived there were some of the original revolutionaries.

Widow wasn't a mountaineer, never trained to be a serious one, but he had trained to climb in the Navy. He knew that Army Rangers used to train in the Presidential Range for mountain warfare. He wasn't sure if they still had a training base there or not. Mountain warfare hasn't been fought in decades. If you don't count Afghanistan, which Widow didn't because Afghan mountains were jagged and deadly, not much climbing was ever needed. If they needed to blow up a Taliban cave, they'd use missiles or helicopters.

Patrols in the mountains stuck to perimeters around forwarding bases or were kept in the mountains that one could hike through.

Plus, in his experience, it took little to get the Taliban to come out of the mountains to do battle. Just announcing that Americans were nearby was usually enough to get them stirred up.

Another thing that he remembered about the Presidential Range was that it had the most diverse weather systems of any place on Earth. It could be very dangerous, which was why many mountaineers trained there before attempting to climb spectral peaks, like K2.

The range has its name because many of the mountains in it are named after presidents and other famous Americans.

Widow moved on and walked northeast; he stuck his thumb out.

He stayed on course to Hellbent, walking along the little shoulder of the track for another thirty minutes, when he heard the slowing of tires, rubber over loose gravel, and the sound of a car with an air conditioner blasting hard inside.

He stopped and looked back to see a vehicle slow, and dust clouds waft from the rear tires. The car stopped five feet from him. The passenger-side tires were over the line on the shoulder, while the driver side tires remained on the track. Not a legal way to come to a stop on a New Hampshire shoulder, but no one was going to say anything to this driver because he was a New Hampshire state trooper in a New Hampshire state patrol car.

The car was a metallic green and tan Dodge Charger that looked more like a park ranger's ride than a trooper's.

The police interceptor package was constructed out of taxpayer money, with every cent accounted for.

Widow could see it all right there.

It was an impressive vehicle.

Homeland Security money combined with federal taxes and state and local, Widow thought. It's got to be spent somewhere.

The Trooper inside wore the state uniform, green shirt, khaki pants. All ironed and pressed and creased like any armed service members would do, but it made Widow think of the Corps.

Marines were the military branch that carried that kind of neatness with them into civilian life. Not all former service members who are neat in civilian life were Marines, but odds were that's what this guy once was.

The Trooper was a man, a young guy, maybe early thirties, with a baby face like he was playing dress-up, overacting as an officer of the law. But he was also a jarhead, which never sits right on a guy with a baby face. It usually made them look younger than they wanted, like infants out of the womb becoming infantry.

Widow smirked at the thought.

At first, the Trooper was on his cell phone, not his radio. He talked for a few extra moments while looking at Widow.

Widow wasn't sure what to do, but was under the distinct impression that he was supposed to wait for the guy to get off the phone, like walking into a gas station and waiting while the attendant spoke to another customer over the store's phone. Even though the standing customer had already pumped his gas, he had to wait for the attendant to get off the phone. No choice. He had to pay for the gas.

Widow thought about just shrugging and turning and walking away. Leave the guy on his phone call. Why not? He had no obligation to stay and wait. He had done nothing wrong. And this was a public road. And the Trooper didn't have his lights on. So why stick around?

Of course, Widow stayed where he was. It wasn't out of a sense of civilian duty or obligation to law enforcement from the state of New Hampshire. He stayed where he was because he didn't have the best track record for first impressions and cops.

The Trooper hung up the phone. He slipped a pair of Ray-Ban sunglasses down the bridge of his nose and stared at Widow over the rims. He looked at Widow from side to side, as if he were reading the tail number off a plane, and then from bottom to top.

The man's blue eyes probed and stared at Widow. Baby-faced or not, the man had cop instincts and cop training and gave Widow a suspicious cop stare. This guy was experienced enough to be formidable. He was a good cop. No question.

Widow could see him remaining friendly, staying calm, keeping a professional demeanor, but the whole time he worked out what to make of Widow, like a bouncer working the door at a nightclub. The guy was threat assessing.

Standard department policy with the public was to remain friendly, but also to stay vigilant when threatened, and Widow was always threatening. He couldn't help it. Threatening was in his DNA, like having blue eyes. It was harder for him to appear friendly with strangers than not.

Terrifying was his default position. No way around it.

Widow aroused suspicion in nearly everyone he encountered daily, especially law enforcement.

The Trooper's nameplate gave his name as Wagner. He buzzed his window down, driver's side. It was automatic. He flicked a switch and waited and leaned his arm out.

Wagner didn't roll down the passenger side. Widow realized the Trooper must've wanted him to walk around to the driver's side. So he did.

The Trooper waited until Widow was standing in full view, three feet from his door, and then he spoke.

"Sir, you okay?"

"I'm good. How's your morning going, Trooper?"

Wagner ignored the question and asked, "Sir, are you broken down out here?"

"Nope."

"What you doing out here, then?"

Widow paused a beat. Because this would cause him a problem. If he told the truth, a red alert would go off in the man's brain. It was just human nature. Typically, people didn't understand why a perfectly able-bodied man would choose a life of wandering around aimlessly. And standing out in the middle of nowhere at a crossroads made him look like a drifter wandering aimlessly.

But what else was he going to say? If he claimed he was going to Hellbent, he'd still look like a hitchhiker, not a real difference between a hitchhiker and a drifter. A hitchhiker was just a drifter with a destination in mind.

So, he kept it simple.

"Walking."

"What's your name, sir?"

"Widow."

He didn't bother giving his first name.

"Are you from Hellbent?"

"No. But I saw Hellbent on a map. And then again on a sign back at the crossroads."

Wagner stayed quiet.

Widow said, "So, what is Hellbent? A town?"

"No. Not really. It's not officially a town. It's more of a place."

Widow stared at him, confusion on his face.

"It's not recognized as a town. There's no mayor or nothing. It's just a community. Technically, it's a part of the county, but the nearest sheriffs are sixty-plus miles north. So, it's my jurisdiction, basically. We consider it a state matter. Somebody's got to look after it."

Widow stayed quiet.

"It's about ten miles north and east. Down this road. In fact, it's the only thing down this road. Unless you're looking to get lost in the wilderness," Wagner said and pointed down the cracked, winding road.

Widow said, "It can't be the only thing?"

"Until Canada, it is."

"Is that so? Can you get to Canada this way?"

Wagner shrugged.

"You can if you're so inclined. It's a treacherous track, though."

"How so?"

"This road only goes to town. There are other roads leading out of town on the other side, but they all lead out into the wilderness, eventually. And out there a man can die. If he doesn't know where the hell he's going."

"Is that a fact?"

"That's a fact."

"You implying I could die out there?"

"You seem not to know where you're going. Not exactly. Could be you."

Widow stayed quiet.

Wagner repeated his question.

"Are you going to Hellbent?"

Widow shrugged.

"Looks that way."

"So, were you going there intentionally?"

"I go nowhere intentionally. If I can help it."

Wagner frowned at that and asked, "Where do you live?"

Widow paused a beat. This question caused him another problem. It always had, when asked by law enforcement. Soon as he told them he didn't live anywhere, he often ended up in a conflict situation. Cops don't like guys without a permanent address: partially, because ordinary people couldn't understand it, and partly, because the most common guys without addresses were criminals evading current warrants calling for their arrest.

Widow wasn't much on telling lies, but he wasn't against it either. Telling lies used to be part of his job description.

"That's where I'm headed."

"Hellbent?"

Widow nodded.

"A second ago, you seemed like you didn't know what I was talking about."

Widow shrugged and gave no answer.

Wagner said, "Well, get in. I'll give you a lift."

Widow paused a beat, stared at the road ahead. Still, no cars were coming. He didn't want to ride with a trooper into town or anywhere else. He preferred to avoid cops and cop cars. They come with handcuffs.

"Come on," Wagner said.

Widow shrugged and stepped around the nose of the car and tried the passenger door handle. It popped back. It was locked.

Widow heard the Trooper's voice, muffled by the glass.

"Get in the back. It's department policy. Civilians ride in the back."

That was what Widow was afraid of.

He stepped to the rear door, opened it, and dumped himself down on the back seat. A bulletproof glass divider separated him from the front, from Wagner. Several pea-sized holes were spread out in the center of the glass in a circular pattern, like a straight on shotgun blast had created them.

Wagner said, "You gotta ride in the back. It's policy."

Widow nodded. It was a policy just about everywhere for non-cops to ride in the back.

The seat was warm, as if it had just been emptied of prisoners. But then Widow realized it was because the air conditioner vents in the back weren't blowing anything. Maybe that was why Wagner had it blasting in the front?

Widow sat and didn't buckle his seatbelt. He stared forward. And felt the car accelerate, slow at first and then hard. It moved forward and a little north and east.

They drove on for about ten more minutes, yet it felt like an eternity because of the dynamics.

Widow was in the back of a cop car, uncomfortable because he hated being under arrest. Even though he wasn't, it all felt the same to him.

3

WAGNER DROVE them both down the cracked, unnamed road until it came to a fork, which was clearly more inviting to the north, which Wagner took.

"What's the other way?"

"That leads to the other side of a lake. There are camp-grounds and hunting cabins out there."

"What kinds of hunting goes on here?"

"Anything."

"Anything?"

"In New Hampshire, it's legal to hunt pretty much anything: deer, moose, even black bear. If you got a license and it's hunting season, then you can kill it."

They drove in silence until Widow tried to make small talk.

He said, "Daniel Webster Highway?"

Wagner kept the car going the less inviting route and said, "Yeah, back there was Daniel Webster Highway. He was from here."

"And Hellbent. And the crossroads."

Wagner stayed quiet.

Widow said, "Is there a story about that? Something to do with the book? Or urban legend?"

"Say what? Urban what?"

Widow turned his head, figured that Wagner didn't get it. So, he just stared out the window and watched the lush green forests go by.

Wagner continued to be on the subject, maybe out of curiosity about what Widow was asking about, but probably because he saw it as an opportunity to discover more about the drifter.

Wagner said, "Daniel Webster was a politician from here. That's why the highway."

Widow just nodded.

"Is that why you were asking?"

"I was asking if there was some kind of reasoning for it."

"For what?"

"For the highway?"

Wagner looked blank.

Widow said, "The crossroads?"

Nothing.

"The town of Hellbent?"

Wagner shook his head. He didn't get it.

"The Devil and Daniel Webster?"

Wagner glanced between the road ahead and the rearview mirror at Widow's reflection.

He asked, "The what? What's the devil got to do with us?"

Widow shook his head slowly and turned back to the window.

"Never mind."

4

THE ROAD LED them between thick, leafy canopies from the branches of substantial northern hardwood trees, which grew on all sides. Low, green carpets of leaves and grass and brush skirted the ground, hiding indigenous woodland creatures, Widow figured. Most of which were harmless rodents, and migrant birds, and probably different species of frogs and lizards. But there were also going to be snakes and bears. And probably mountain lions or some kinds of wild cats.

Wagner had slowed because most of the road was covered in muddy rain puddles left from the night before, Widow guessed.

The sun became sparse for several seconds as they drove through the thick of the forest, until they exited the forest and came to rolling hills and the first sign of human life, which occurred as a gas station. Two of them. One across from the other. Both major competitors. Both corporate oil and gas companies that Widow had heard of before and weren't going away soon. Both stations were old but well-kept. Both with equal prices per gallon down to the fractions of a penny marked high on signs.

Both stations had large pumps around the back, down empty service roads, accommodating for trucks, but major freight trucks didn't come through here. Wagner had told him that the roads on the other side of town sprawled out in the wilderness. No vehicles would drive through there to Canada.

Then Widow saw a truck pulling out from one of the large pumping areas and exiting down the attached service road.

It hauled a long trailer with a bed full of tied-down lumber, which was wet as if it had been sitting out all night in the rain or it had been covered by a tarp that couldn't stand the hard winds and blew away.

Widow watched it for a while and then turned back to the town ahead.

Hellbent must've had a lumber mill, made sense. It was probably a distribution center for local timber. There were plenty of trees out there.

Wagner had mentioned a lake, which probably meant a river system somewhere. Widow was unfamiliar with lumber mill life, but he knew loggers used rivers like pipelines, to transport felled trees downstream until they made it to the mill to be shredded and cut down to manageable lumber sizes. And then they were transported by truck or train to other destinations.

Wagner drove them over a hill, and Widow saw a unique and quaint settlement, which was just as Wagner had described it, small and paltry enough not to be considered a town. But there it was. And it had a sign, which was posted up high on two wooden poles, painted white like an upside-down field goal post.

A massive block sign, all wood, all etched letters, read: Welcome to Hellbent.

The sign was bent back, pushed back by decades of harsh wind blowing in from the south. Widow could hear the wind, even though the windows in the trooper's Charger were all rolled up.

He could see it when he looked east to the closest trees. The leaves blew hard like green candle flames, dancing in the wind.

Widow took in the terrain. There were mountains to the far south, trees everywhere, rolling green hills, mud puddles, and dampness everywhere, but the sky was blue and clear. There were more mountains to the north and a small gothic settlement called: Hellbent, right smack in the middle.

Wagner saw Widow checking it all out and said, "It's like a Cole painting, right?"

"Who?"

"Thomas Cole. He lived around here. A famous painter who painted the White Mountains."

Widow nodded, said, "Landscapes."

"Yeah. Beautiful landscapes. He was a good man."

"Hitler also painted landscapes," Widow muttered.

"What's that?"

"Nothing. Where you planning to drop me off?"

"I gotta check in with the local marshal."

"Marshal? There's a US Marshal's office? Here?"

"No. It's just the local lawman's title."

"What like in the Old West?"

"Sure. Some communities are too small for official police departments and deputies and the spending of taxpayer money to provide such services. That's why I drive through here once a week."

"Too small? There are two gas stations."

"This county has nothing but this town. People have to drive long distances to work. Out here, the main industry is timber. The mills are spread way out there."

Widow nodded.

"How many marshals are there?"

"There's only one. She has a volunteer deputy. And that's it."

Widow nodded.

They stopped at a four-way stop sign and turned onto the main street. Widow saw a pharmacy, a local market, a church combined with a firehouse, and a taxidermist. It was weird, but so far, nothing about Hellbent was normal.

"The place looks big enough to be considered an official town."

"It has grown in the last twenty years. They review it every couple."

"And?"

"Like I mentioned. The state officials' main concern is providing the taxpaying services here. New Hampshire's budget is spread pretty thin these days."

Widow nodded. State governments were more reckless than the federal government, which was surprising, and not.

On the other side of the street, everything was laid out a little more uneven. There were a few bars and empty businesses that used to be something. Most of them still had faded paint where signs used to be posted.

There was another side street with motels, all well-maintained. All small chains that Widow had heard of. All the parking lots were full.

"What's with all the full motel lots?"

Wagner glanced over and then back at the road.

"The timber mills. Many of the workers are migrants. They end up staying in those motels like apartments. Which basically they are. The owners just never upgraded."

"They got any empty rooms?"

"How would I know?"

They took a turn, and a street left and then a hard right and passed more shops. One was a barber, which Widow made a note of because he needed a haircut and a decent shave.

They came to a three-way stop sign, and Wagner made a complete, full stop as if he was setting an example for Widow. They were coming off the single street, so Wagner looked both ways. Widow followed suit, an involuntary habit.

No cars came from either direction.

Widow faced forward.

"You can let me out here."

Wagner stayed quiet. He paused a little longer than necessary at the stop sign. He looked back at Widow in the rearview, and his lips moved, but he said nothing and looked forward and drove off.

After a long, uncomfortable moment, Widow said, "Did you hear me?"

Wagner was quiet.

Widow spoke up. Not shouting or demanding, but in a firm voice. He put some extra bass in his voice, making him sound like a retired cop, which he was, basically.

"Did you hear me?"

"Oh, yeah, I heard ya."

"So, what's the deal?"

"I'm glad to give you a lift into town, Mr. Widow. But I'm not a taxi. I'm afraid you're going where I'm going. You can get out there."

"And where the hell are you going?"

"Like I said, I'm headed to meet with the town marshal. From there, you can go wherever you'd like."

Great, Widow thought. Once again, he was in the back of a police car, against his will, and headed straight for jail. Even though he wasn't being arrested, not yet.

They drove on another dawdling mile, half straight, half turns, and they came to a laundromat. It was a sad, two-story building that looked like it had existed since the Revolutionary War.

They had thrown paint over the original masonry brick several times over the last century.

What surprised Widow was that Wagner stopped the car right in front of the laundromat. He moved in his seat, adjusting his height, and rechecked the rearview. Then he K-turned the Charger and pulled the car into a side street. He stopped directly behind an F-150 pickup and put the Charger into park.

"This is it."

"This is what?"

"This is our stop."

"A laundromat?"

"That's just the first floor."

Widow cocked his head and stared out at a set of metal stairs leading up to an external door on a second-floor platform. The stairs looked like an inner-city fire escape.

"So what? The Hellbent police station is on the top of a laundromat?"

"Times're tight, Mr. Widow. The local marshal's literally a one-woman show. And like I said about the state affairs, this woman ain't even got a budget."

A woman town marshal, Widow thought. That was something the Old West never had, not to his knowledge.

Wagner killed the engine and got out. He opened Widow's door.

Widow stepped out and stood there as Wagner shut the door behind him.

"You headed any place in particular?"

"I could use a haircut."

Widow waited, expecting Wagner to point him back in the barbershop's direction they passed, with helpful instructions on where to turn, what street was a shortcut, but he never did.

Instead, right then, a heavy door at the top of the stairs scraped open, pulling inward, and an old-fashioned bell rigged to the top corner of the door dinged, an anemic sound, probably loud enough to alert whoever was present upstairs that a visitor had arrived. But it worked both ways, only weak on this side.

Widow watched as a woman climbed out onto the landing. She paused a brief second and then descended the stairs. She was dressed in a casual uniform with the settlement's name written on a khaki button-down shirt, right there on her right breast pocket.

There was no official title for her—no Sheriff's Department. No Police. No Marshal. The shirt was just a shirt.

On the left breast pocket was a nameplate, gold, not silver. It read her name, still no title. As Widow read it to himself, Wagner said it and added to it.

"Widow, this is Marshal Jo Bridges."

Widow stayed still for a moment, but then he reached his hand out for her to shake.

Jo Bridges was a rough- and tough-looking woman. Physically, she was a woman, no doubt about that. She had a combination build that was a cross between roller derby queen and a tennis player with some extra added layers from her age and occupation. She wore no makeup and sported a shaved head, which didn't look bad on her. She had that kind of helmet-shaped head that supported a bald look well.

Her shirt was perfectly ironed, but her jeans looked slept in, and maybe a day old since she first whipped them out of a closet or a dryer.

Widow guessed that like Wagner, Bridges had once been military, but much farther back in time than Wagner. She had signs of someone disciplined by military life who had been out for so long that civilian casualness had taken over.

She said, "Good to meet you, Widow."

"Likewise."

And then, out of the blue, she asked a question that told Widow exactly what this was.

It was a setup.

She asked, "So what's your business here in Hellbent?"

Widow thought back to when Wagner first picked him up. He was on the phone. A quick call. Who was he talking to?

It had been Bridges. He had probably called ahead, told her about a guy looking lost, standing in the mouth of her jurisdiction.

That's why Wagner hadn't let him out at the three-way stop. He wasn't just giving Widow a friendly lift into town. He was bringing him directly to the local marshal so she could get a good look at him, just like in the days of the Old West. He was the one stranger, walking into town. She was the town marshal who didn't like trouble in her town. She was sizing him up to see if he was going to be trouble for her or not.

Widow said, "I got no business."

"You got no business here?"

He looked onward and shrugged.

"I got no business anywhere."

This answer seemed to annoy her for a moment.

"What're you doing here? Before you say that Wagner brought you here, like some kind of smartass. Remember, right now, I'm asking you nicely. I expect an actual answer."

Wagner said, "Show some respect, Widow."

Widow didn't react to this. It seemed like Wagner was interjecting to be included or he was playing bad cop.

Widow stayed quiet for a moment and made it look like he was lost in thought, but he wasn't.

He couldn't care less about whatever they were up to.

But eventually, he'd have to play along if he wanted to avoid trouble.

So, he told her. He told them both—all the highlights. He told them he used to be in the Navy, but wasn't anymore. He mentioned he used to be NCIS, to garner favor as one cop to another, but he left out the top-secret, classified status of his unit and his undercover work and his SEAL ops.

He also told them that once he was pulled out of the service because of a death in the family, he stayed out, and had been wandering aimlessly for the past few years.

Both cops looked at each other and then at Widow.

Bridges asked, "You're homeless?"

Widow sighed. He guessed that his previous service counted for nothing. Not anymore. Not to these two. Not in the back of beyond.

"Technically, yes. I'm homeless."

They paused a beat.

Bridges looked like she was contemplating something. It was probably what to make of Widow. She couldn't arrest him, not for doing anything wrong. And she couldn't kick him out of town, although she could, just not legally.

Impasse.

Wagner looked like he was merely waiting for her instructions.

She was the lower rank in terms of cops and state law enforcement agencies, but she was the ranking officer in terms of experience.

She had fifteen-plus years on Wagner.

Bridges took a step back, and Wagner followed. They turned their backs to Widow and whispered to each other for a long minute.

Widow asked, "What the hell is this?"

They turned and stepped back.

Bridges said, "In the last few days, we've had some new arrivals."

"New arrivals?"

"Outsiders. That's all. New people."

"And that's got something to do with me?"

"Five hundred twenty people live in this town, Widow. We've got nothing to see. No tourist business to speak of. Except during hunting season, which legally doesn't start here for another thirty days. And every year, we get the same people who show up here to hunt without fail. The same guys come. They stay. They hunt. They leave."

"And?"

"And in the last three days, I've seen about a dozen new faces that I ain't never seen before."

"So? Word gets around. You got a lot of wilderness out here. And quiet. And no one lives here. Don't hunters like that?"

"The new faces aren't hunters."

Wagner said, "They look like bikers."

"Bikers?"

"Bikers," Bridges said, "You know rough guys on motorcycles, like a gang."

"Last night, there was a fire out in the woods."

Widow asked, "You think the bikers started the fire?"

"No idea. I haven't seen the fire yet. I just got the report this morning."

Wagner said, "That's why I'm here. We're going to go check it out now."

"No one went to have a look last night?"

They said nothing.

Widow said, "There might've been someone in need of help?"

Wagner said, "I don't know what part of the state you were in last night, but here it was pouring rain."

Widow could see that. He already noticed the puddles. There was one close to him.

"Still, isn't it your duty to protect and serve?"

Bridges raised a hand and rested it on her holstered sidearm, like a signal telling Widow to watch his mouth.

Wagner noticed it too but didn't repeat the action. Maybe he was more willing to think for himself than Widow had given him credit for.

Bridges didn't respond with a direct answer to Widow's comment.

"Most likely, it's a meth lab that got too hot."

"Meth and bikers go hand in hand. They usually are in the business of addictive, illegal substances."

Bridges said, "It happens out here at least once a year."

Wagner said, "Small community. Bikers take up residence here. Some of them come from local families. Families with nothing to do. Bills to pay. They cook meth."

Widow said, "Sounds like it's a family business. It sounds like you already got a suspect."

"No suspects. Not till we take a look. But the thing is, the motorcycle gang that used to be here. We haven't seen them in months."

"So, what happened to them?"

Bridges shrugged.

"They up and left. Probably expanding business to better grounds. Not a lot of money to be made out here. Not compared to other territories. But we still got some folks out here cooking."

"Why haven't you cracked down on them?"

Bridges shot Widow a look that said: Who the hell are you to ask me that?

"There's a fine balance in a small community like this. Like an ecosystem. A certain amount of criminal element is tolerated. It's expected. It's the way things are."

Widow didn't like that answer, but he said nothing. Not his town. Not his job. Not his problem.

Bridges said, "Besides, they keep to themselves, mostly. There are the people who cook it and the ones who buy it, and it stays that way—a cycle. We don't have it in our schools or nothing. It stays out there."

She pointed with her free hand and waved it over an area of wilderness to the north and swept it over the east.

"As long as it stays out there, I don't really care. I'm only one cop. I can't be starting a drug war on my own with the families out there. They'd win anyway."

Widow said, "So, call the DEA?"

"We've tried."

"And?"

"They're busy. This is small-time. And the agencies of the government see us as a bunch of backwoods people. The DEA won't lift a finger for a bunch of backwoods people."

Wagner said, "Plus, they keep blowing themselves up."

"Sounds like they're not good meth cooks. If they keep blowing themselves up."

Bridges smiled and moved her hand away from her gun.

Widow noticed.

Silence.

In the distance, Widow heard the backfire of a truck and tires on pavement and the wind rustling between the buildings.

He looked at Wagner, thought back to when he was first picked up at the crossroads.

Wagner was on the phone with someone. He'd bet it was Bridges. He was probably telling her that a stranger was walking to Hellbent.

Widow turned to Wagner.

"Let me guess. You've got an influx of bikers coming in for the first time—new faces. And you thought I might be one of them? That's why you brought me here. So that she could get a look at me?"

Wagner said, "Don't take it personally."

"We just needed to know what we're dealing with here."

Widow said, "I'm not a threat. I'm not part of a biker gang. Or a meth business."

He paused a beat. They waited.

"You know how you can tell?"

They both looked at him with suspicion still all over their faces.

"I don't have a motorcycle."

They said nothing to that.

Widow stepped back, noticeably. He got five feet away and stopped and looked at Wagner.

"Thanks for the ride," he said.

And he turned to walk away.

Wagner started to protest, but, in the end, he didn't.

There was nothing to say.

Widow walked away into the sunlight.

5

Sitting in a barber's chair, Widow had a clear line of sight out the barbershop window to the street outside and to the storefronts and roads mapping the terrain beyond that.

Most of Hellbent's streets were old, but clean and maintained from their original New England gothic style. Everything had a lived-in feel.

Widow stared at cars passing and looked over freshly cut grass and small bricked storefronts. He saw a post office, a dentist, a bakery, a nail salon, and one lone building with a glass-blowing business.

There was one empty plot that was a small playground for kids.

He saw young children playing.

Like the town's streets, the playground equipment was old. The equipment was all metal and dated. There were bare-bones monkey bars. There was a swing set with a small section of plastic animal swings, one horse and one lion. The slide was metal, and the seesaw was made of wood.

All of it old, but with fresh coats of paint.

To the east side of the park was a single building, a train depot. It was equipped with a platform, all wood. It was set up on a hill.

Widow asked the barber two simple questions, just making small talk. And right then, at that moment, he asked them. They were both answered without the barber having to say a word. But he did anyway.

Widow asked, "The train ever come through?"

"Oh, sure."

"It ever stop?"

Right then, they both heard a train whistle, faint and distant at first, until it bellowed again and again.

The barber stayed busy at work, trimming the grown-out hair that was like weeds.

Widow angled his head to get a better look.

"Keep still," the barber said.

Widow stayed quiet and stayed angled.

He looked at the train. Maybe it was his overpowering sense of curiosity that made him look. Maybe it was the cop instincts that never seemed to go away. Maybe it was boredom from sitting in that chair. Or maybe it was just that he wondered who the hell would come out here?

Why would Amtrak even have a stop here?

The train slowed. The rails sang, winding down to a slow rhythmic pulse, and then to nothing.

The train crawled forward past the platform until the third car was lined up at the end of the station, and the train stopped completely, rocking forward once and shifting back into a safe disembarking position. It tarried there, still for a long moment, as if the engineer was making a hard choice and having second thoughts about it.

The barber started on the sides of Widow's head with a pair of clippers. The clippers hummed and buzzed in Widow's ears. The buzzing overrode the train's slowing sounds, and he heard no more from it.

He watched as the train doors on the third car finally opened. No other doors opened. And no one got off for another long moment. Finally, someone did.

He watched a petite figure step off the train, carefully. Not as though the steps were hard for her to take, but more out of caution. Once she set foot on the platform, she moved fast and gracefully, like a ballet dancer. No problem.

Still, there was something different about her. Something a little awkward about her step, a little off pace, a little off-kilter. She moved like a ballet dancer who just got off a long horse ride, or like she might've been hit in the head, and she was still getting used to dancing with a head injury.

She moved like a Marine humping gear up a hill, and it was getting too heavy for him to carry.

With his head angled the way it was, and with the barber moving in and out of his line of sight, it was hard for Widow to put his finger on what her deal was at first.

The barber continued to clip the sides of Widow's hair until finally bringing out the scissors and using both tools at once.

The train rocked back on its wheels for a moment, and then the engine droned loud enough for Widow to hear over the clippers. The horn blasted a couple more times, and the train rocked forward again. This time it moved away from its stop.

No one else got off the train.

Widow watched it roll away.

The tracks *boomed*, and the rails sang for a long second more. Eventually, the train moved clear out of sight.

The lone, disoriented ballet woman stood there, scoping out the town. She scanned the buildings and the streets, looking like she had no idea where she was or what direction she would go in.

Then Widow noticed. She had a carry-on bag, small and hooked over her shoulder by two straps. It wasn't a purse. Just an everyday black canvas bag. Nothing fancy.

There was still something out of the norm about her. Suddenly, she looked right and looked left, like she was deciding, and she walked left.

She turned and walked.

Widow saw from her profile the thing that was causing her to walk a little unevenly, the thing that made her like a Marine tired from humping heavy gear. He saw she was humping extra gear, after all.

By the time the lone ballet woman stepped off the platform, Widow saw why she had taken slow steps, why she had been a little off-balance.

He watched her walk steadily to the middle of the platform. She stood there, looked left again, and looked right again, then she pulled her left hand out and up above her breasts and twisted her wrist and stared at a watch that she wore upside down, which struck Widow with a sense of military familiarity.

After checking the time, she lowered her wrist back down to her side and repeated the scanning of the left and right process a third time, perhaps searching for someone who was supposed to meet her, someone who was supposed to pick her up. That someone wasn't there, not where he or she was supposed to be.

Cars passed on the street in front of the barbershop, blocking Widow's view every so often. But the woman stayed on the platform longer, in sight.

She was small in stature. She stood maybe five-foot-nothing with a long neck, looking like she had spent a lifetime staring up at people taller than she and her body grew the neck to accommodate, like a giraffe needing to have a long neck to reach the tops of trees.

For being so short, the woman was almost all legs. She had long, toned legs that doubled Widow's suspicions that she was some sort of dancer or runner or gymnast, or all three.

She had medium-length black hair that looked to be growing out. As she turned, Widow saw one side of her hair was shaved above and behind her ear, right down to dark stubble. It was what he'd call a punk rocker look. Only her clothes weren't the same style, not really.

She wore a pair of blue jean overalls with shorts instead of pants, all underneath a black leather jacket.

The jacket served sixty percent for style because it was summer, but also New Hampshire summers up in the mountains were quite windy. And this summer was no different. The jacket served forty percent for the function of keeping her warm.

There was something else very notable about her. It was the factor that made her walk a little awkwardly, a little cumbersome.

The woman on the platform was very pregnant.

Widow watched her for another thirty seconds while she walked to the stairs, off the platform and down to the street. No one appeared to meet her. There was no driver waiting to pick her up, no husband waiting to greet her. No family. No one.

After another moment of standing there with a lost look on her face, she turned left and vanished from sight.

6

THE DRIVE OUT to the reported cabin fire took Bridges and Wagner over thirty minutes, partly because it was way out in the mountains. Also partly because the rain from the night before had muddied the ground, and most of the roads out that way were dirt, which promptly turned to mud, which was drying back to the soil.

The other reason was that the wilderness was immense. There was lots of land with few signs of life.

Hellbent was a small town, but Bridges' jurisdiction was a massive section of the county because it was wilderness, mountains, small lakes, and not much else.

Most of the citizens of Hellbent lived in or near town. Most of the farms were within the first ten miles back to town.

Rural people lived this far out, including low-income families, meth heads, and misers, people who just wanted to be left alone.

Bridges knew all of them. She made it a routine to call the ones who had phones, and the few who didn't, she'd drive all the way out to visit once every other month. One guy lived the farthest out. He was so far out that she only saw him once or twice a year. And he usually came riding down from the mountains on horseback into town. He would stop in and say hello.

All the guys who lived way, way out were men. No families. No women. No children. Just unattached men who enjoyed being alone.

They rode out in Bridges' truck. No way would Wagner's Charger make it out on the rockier roads. Plus, if they got stuck in the mud, Bridges' truck had a winch mounted on the front.

Wagner peered forward and said, "I still don't see any smoke."

"The rain put it out last night, I guess."

The pickup truck's tires dragged them easily over wet dirt and loose gravel. The windows were rolled down. They were up in altitude over the town. Cold, dry air blew in from the mountains.

"How many cabins are out here, anyway?" Wagner asked.

"You don't want to know."

Wagner smiled and reached over to a cup holder on the console. He pulled up a coffee thermos and drank from it.

"Can't believe you don't like coffee," he said.

Bridges didn't look at him. She kept her focus on the bumpy terrain coming up. Her hands were covered by driving gloves. Wagner didn't understand that. Her truck wasn't anything special. But he didn't question her about it because he knew a lot of officers who wore gloves. He always chalked it up to being germaphobes.

He couldn't blame her. In their line of work, sometimes they dealt with the lowest common denominator, like the meth head bikers she'd mentioned to that stranger, Widow. And meth heads weren't known for being the most sanitary citizens.

They drove on, and Wagner asked, "So what's the next cabin on the list?"

She looked over at him this time.

"Actually, I'm not sure."

"Not sure?"

"A fire in the middle of the wilderness, at a log cabin, we assumed it was meth."

"And what? It's not?"

She shrugged, looked back at the road.

"We've already seen almost a dozen cabins."

"And?"

"And those are all the ones that the bikers used for cooking. Plus, I haven't seen that gang in a while."

"Are they still operating out here?"

"I don't know. The only two left are the vape boys."

Vape wasn't their name. It was a nickname because their family owned a vape store in town.

"Maybe they cleared out. Maybe it's just some new local outfit, trying to make money and having no clue how dangerous it is."

"Maybe."

"Maybe they have a cabin you don't know about?"

"Maybe."

They were quiet for a moment.

Bridges said, "Maybe, it's not a meth lab."

"In that case, one of our more upstanding citizens could be in real trouble."

She nodded and said, "There's a hunter's cabin up here. Let's stop there."

7

AFTER THE HAIRCUT and a close shave, Widow wanted to grab a late breakfast. He was starving. He thanked the barber and tipped him, and asked for the best diner in town with the best breakfast. Judging by the barrel of a stomach the barber was sporting, he would know the answer to that question. He'd know about the best breakfast, the best lunch, and the best dinner. And it seemed he did because he pointed Widow south, back part of the way he had come and a little west, claiming that a local diner had the "best eggs scrambled this side of the Mississippi," his words.

Afterward, the barber thanked Widow for the tip. Nothing too polite or beholden, the guy just expressed the amount of politeness and gratitude that was expected. No more. No less.

Widow left the barbershop and followed the man's instructions, and turned left and walked in a southern direction. The buildings, the streets, even the gutters, were all picturesque and quaint as if they came from a poem about nineteen-fifties America.

He passed a coffee shop that was tempting, but he was eager to try the recommended diner and compare the scrambled eggs with the ones from his memories.

He walked past an ice cream shop, law office, a food stop, and another haircut place, but this one was a salon and had women inside near the front windows, curlers in their hair, and some under dome helmet industrial dryers.

Two of the women approached the window, pressed their hands against the glass, and stared at him like he was a gorilla who had escaped from the nearest zoo.

He carried on and passed a sports bar that was closed. There was a pet grooming place that doubled as a kennel. He heard dogs barking from behind the brick walls and double-glass doors.

All the shops were attached at the walls like brownstones. They were painted different shades of the same four colors. All of them were brick.

Widow stopped when he came to something he had not seen before in a small place like this. It was another shop, but this one stuck out as different, as something unique in a small place.

It was a vape shop. These vape shops were steadily replacing the old cigar smoke shops that used to be more common. Vaping was a young industry, compared to all the other more established places. It might've even been invented in the twenty-first century. He wasn't sure.

Out front, he saw a teal Dodge truck. It was old, but he saw no rust. It wasn't pristine either. Mud and dirt were caked under the wheel wells and splashed across the bumper, which had a small dent in it.

Widow figured the owner had been driving out on dirt roads this morning. Maybe the mud and dirt were direct results of the previous night's rain.

Widow crossed the street over to that side and walked on the sidewalk.

An elderly couple, not ancient, but nearing the age of retirement and senior discounts, came out of the vape store. They weren't arguing, but having a vocal discussion like old couples do.

The man said, "Dorothy, get off my back. I don't know why they're not here."

"They're not here 'cause they were probably out getting drunk last night."

"I'm here. So, let's get these boxes in."

"You can't lift those boxes."

The man ignored her and let the Dodge's tailgate down. He bent slightly and tried to scoop up a single box out of the back of the truck.

He dropped it the moment after he lifted it.

Widow came up behind them.

"Can I help you guys with that?"

He helped the man out of the way.

"Do you guys want all three boxes inside?"

The woman named Dorothy said, "Yes. Thanks for helping us."

"No problem."

Widow lifted the dropped box off the tailgate and stacked it on top of the next, and then stacked those on top of the third. He lifted all three. Not too heavy, just bulky, and hard to maneuver.

"Can you get all that?" Dorothy asked.

"Not a problem. Just guide me to where you need them."

"This way," she said.

Widow used his head to help prop them up, and he craned his neck like a turtle so that he could see around the side of the stack.

He followed her voice.

"Right this way," she said.

She propped open a door for him. Then he heard an electric buzz from a bell. It was one of those that notified shopkeepers of someone opening their street door, an upgrade from the ancient bell at the marshal's laundromat office.

He passed through the door, slowly, and followed Dorothy over to a spot near a glass countertop that displayed dozens of types of vape pens and cartridges and carrying cases and other knickknacks for collectors and vapers. Widow had no idea what most of them were or what they were for.

"Set it down there."

Widow set the stack of boxes down on the countertop and backed away. Out of desire to be polite, he acted like the whole ordeal was taxing, which it wasn't. It was an attempt to allow the man to save face and save pride in front of his wife, like the reason he couldn't lift the boxes wasn't that he was too old to be lifting heavy boxes, but it was that the boxes were very heavy. Any younger man would've had the same trouble lifting them.

Widow was different because he was a giant. Nature had given him a cheat code. How could her husband compete with that?

"Well, thank you, stranger," Dorothy said.

"That was nice of you, mister," the man said.

Widow nodded a polite nod and introduced himself.

"Widow. First name, Jack."

He reached his hand out, offering a friendly handshake to the man first, and then to Dorothy.

"Bill and this is my wife, Dorothy."

"Nice to meet you both."

They all shook hands.

"Can we do something for you?" Bill asked.

Dorothy said, "To thank you for helping us? Would you like a vape pen?"

The man turned and elbowed Dorothy in the arm. Nothing hard, not anything close to spousal abuse. It was more of a lifetime affair.

Like he was saying, *Hey, don't give away the store!*

"No, ma'am. Thanks for the offer, but I don't vape. I don't understand the appeal of it."

"It's a cleaner, healthier alternative to smoking cigarettes."

"So it helps you quit? I don't need help to quit. I quit a long time ago."

"No. It's not for quitting," Bill added.

"It helps, but vaping is its own thing. It's not about quitting smoking. Although, that's why half of our customers do it."

"Either way, no thanks. I've got a vice already."

They looked at him sideways for a moment.

"What vice do you have?" she asked.

Bill muttered, "Probably steroids."

Widow thought, *It's coffee.*

At which point, Widow saw another elbow thrown in this marriage, only this one was from Dorothy at Bill. It was hard and landed right on his side, under his right arm. He let out a gasp and grabbed at his side.

Widow imagined that over the course of their marriage, which he guessed to be in the double digits, year-wise, there had been many elbows thrown from each of them at the other, no innocent party there, guilt on both sides, like a long-standing family feud that no one could remember who started or why or over what, and just as trivial at this point.

The whole thing was now a family tradition.

Widow cracked a smile. This was married life. He didn't get it, but it was endearing.

Bill grabbed his side like it hurt, which it did. She had let him have it hard, much harder than he did to her.

"Are you sure you want nothing?" Dorothy repeated.

Widow thought for a moment and came back with his answer.

"I'm a sailor. Former sailor."

She stared at him blankly.

Widow said, "I was in the Navy. We dealt in intel. We can trade, the labor for some intel?"

The blank stare continued.

Widow said, "We can trade information."

She nodded.

"What kind of information do you need?"

"Two things only."

She nodded again.

"The first is out of curiosity. How's business for a vape store in a place like this?"

"Business is real good."

"Really?"

Dorothy moved closer and leaned her back against the counter. Her sleeves jerked up on her shirt, and Widow saw an old, faded tattoo. Couldn't tell what it had been because the ink had long ago needed touched up.

She put her hands up to her lips and cupped it around like she was blocking someone from lip-reading what she was about to say.

"Oh yeah. It's better than more non-legal means of making money. Believe me. We got out of that game."

She had said non-legal and not illegal, like it was a way of covering up that she meant not legal.

Widow nodded along.

"Dorothy, don't talk about that."

"It's okay. I'm not the law."

Bill nodded.

"We know that. Hellbent's only got one cop."

Silence.

Widow wondered what the criminal industry that they had once been in was? Drugs were the obvious answer.

Dorothy said, "The vape business is very good out here because other than work and fishing and hunting, there's not much left for people to do, except drink and smoke.

"Vape is a lot better option than other things people like to smoke."

Drugs were the answer to what criminal activity they had once been in before.

Bill fidgeted like he was uncomfortable with his wife being so blasé about sharing this private family information with a total stranger. He interrupted.

"Mr. Widow, what's the other information you need?"

"I was told that Mable's Diner had the best eggs in town."

Bill nodded.

Dorothy said, "That's not true."

"It is so, Dorothy," Bill said.

"It's not. They're the same eggs that everyone has. We all buy them from the same market, Bill."

"Don't pay attention to her. Mable's has the best."

Widow said, "I was told the scrambled eggs are great."

"No, don't get the scrambled. Get the New England omelet. That's their best meal with eggs."

Widow nodded, recorded the information in his head.

"So, which way is it? I was told to keep heading this way."

He pointed at the wall to his left.

"That's right. Just keep going that way. You can't miss it."

After that, Widow thanked both Dorothy and Bill in that order, and they returned the pleasantries and thanked him for helping with the boxes.

He headed out the door, back to his mission to find breakfast.

On the street, he stopped and saw two big Harley Davidsons riding in from the other direction.

Two huge boys rode on the back of them. They weren't older than Widow. They were younger, not much younger, but they both looked ten years older. Widow's guess was hard-living, smoking meth, from what he was to understand from Wagner and Bridges, and now Bill and Dorothy.

The hogs they rode exhausted smoke and roared in a low, lion-like rumble. The motorcyclists rode up slowly. When they noticed him, they plowed ahead, fast.

They came up and passed the vape store, beyond the old, parked Dodge, and rode a little way past Widow. Then they both stopped up on a hill right in the intersection ahead of him. They circled around, each going the opposite direction. They exchanged positions and came back down toward him.

The two boys stopped alongside him in the road and rumbled the bikes louder and louder, like apes discovering an intruder in their jungle.

Widow knew little about motorcycles. Being honest with himself, the only reason he knew these were Harley Davidsons was that the company had an iconic logo, which he saw on the bikes. But then he figured that these two biker wannabes could've just slapped Harley Davidson stickers on the fuel tanks.

Either way, the bikers stopped and turned their heads in his direction. One of them took a pair of Oakley sunglasses off his face, let them drop to hang from a cord around his neck. The second biker followed suit, but kept his sunglasses folded over a big gloved hand.

"Hey, boy. You got a reason to be here?"

Boy? No one had called him boy since he was a boy.

"What business is that of yours?"

Widow stepped right and back, a foot away from the curb. The shadow from the top corner of the building behind him fell over his body and vision, allowing him to get a better look at the bikers' faces.

He saw they were related. Probably brothers, but maybe cousins.

What was it that Bridges and Wagner had told him? Local motorcycle clubs cook and sell meth. So, maybe these guys were a part of that motorcycle club. Perhaps they were interested in him because of the way he looked, being an outsider, just like Wagner and Bridges had taken him.

Often Widow was mistaken for a criminal, more than he ever was as a cop. Which worked well for him back then, but now it was getting tiresome.

The one that Widow guessed to be the older brother spoke.

"Boy, you playing smart? I'm asking you a question."

Widow said, "I don't answer to you. I don't even have to talk to you if I don't want to."

"Is that so?"

"That's so. In fact, if I choose, I could just cross this street and go on my way."

The younger brother repeated basically the same question.

"That right?"

"That's right."

The two brothers stared at him, calculating, processing, considering the right course of action to take.

Widow stepped left and forward, back into the light. He had already plotted his course. He was crossing the street, with or without putting these two in the dirt.

Just then, Bill and Dorothy stepped outside their store. Bill stopped at his truck until he saw what was happening on the street corner, and then he started walking up the sidewalk toward Widow.

The two brothers stayed on their bikes and looked at Bill.

Bill stopped halfway to Widow and called out.

"What the hell are you boys doing?"

That's when things changed completely.

The younger brother spoke first.

"We're not doing anything, sir."

The older one said, "We're just checking up on this guy. He was loitering around the store."

Widow noticed the guy had said the store and not your store like the store belonged to him just as much as it did to Bill and Dorothy. But then Widow noticed a particular change in status, a change in demeanor, a retreat from the apelike activity that they had been demonstrating. Now he was looking at a different set of bikers threatening him. Now, he was looking at two timid, overgrown children.

And the younger one had said, sir.

They were Bill and Dorothy's boys.

Bill spoke again.

"That's Jack Widow, boys. He's our friend. Now, let him cross."

The bikers looked at Widow, slipped their Oakleys back on, and backed off.

Dorothy came up to join her husband. She called out to the bikers.

"Lads, are you bothering Mr. Widow?"

Lads? Widow thought. Must be a pet name like Junior or Bubba.

"No, ma'am," they said in unison.

She put two judgmental hands on her hips, a move that only a mother does when correcting her offspring.

The two bikers were Bill and Dorothy's sons. No question.

Widow smiled and spoke.

"Guess I'll be on my way then, lads."

Widow stepped off the curb, checked both ways, and crossed the street, ignoring the sons and moving on.

8

HELLBENT, whether it was a town, a city, a community, a commune, or just a spot on a map, was wholly misnamed. So far, it was the farthest thing from hell or any semblance of a demonic town.

To Widow, the place seemed like an ideal destination in the fall to watch the leaves and the foliage for city folks who were into that sort of thing.

Widow walked past a short row of tourist shops and streets with plenty of wooded areas, until he saw a road called Ignominy Avenue, which was another unusual name. Ignominy was a word that described a type of shame or disgrace. It was like the avenue was named to show a black mark on Hellbent's history.

Widow being Widow, he turned onto it and followed the street, which wound down into a residential area.

Charismatic, timeworn Victorian houses lined the block with picket fences and big trees. Leaves fluttered slowly like the opening shot of a movie. Cars lined the street, parked. Not one of them newer than ten years, but all of them well-kept, as if they had just been purchased at a used car lot.

Widow thought about the directions given by the barber. According to his calculations, he could continue on Ignominy Avenue and stroll down one block, take a left and wind up at Mable's Diner.

It was a gamble, but a scenic one—a better payoff. Widow walked casually down the street. He stepped off the sidewalk and strolled down the middle of the road, staying on the white line. He did this to get a broader view.

He walked on for ten more minutes until he saw the oddest thing. Right in the middle of Ignominy Avenue was a median, which was normal. But it was overgrown with grass and weeds and one lone tree. There was a section, in front of the tree, closed off by a short, rusted, wrought-iron fence. The iron plotted out a section of ground about ten feet by ten feet.

The thing that was so odd about it was that at the center of the squared plot of land, surrounded by the wrought-iron fence, under the tree, covered in the tree's shadow, was an untended, forgotten grave.

9

JUST OVER THE brim of a gully that was carved out centuries ago, one of Major's guys, not Attack Dog, but one just as loyal and just as deadly, but less than reliable, sat on his motorcycle like a cowboy would have sat on a horse's saddle more than a hundred years before.

Both of his legs were extended outward. He used them as side stands to brace the bike. The engine was on, idling and humming in a low rumble.

From his saddlebag, he pulled out a pair of field glasses. He stared through them at the police truck climbing the trail back to the cabin.

His job had been to return the next morning and scope it out. He was to make sure that everything was destroyed. That there was no evidence remaining. Dead, burned corpses were fine, but not left in the positions that they had left them in. He was to make sure the bones were dragged and piled inside where the cabin had been.

But he had messed up. He was supposed to be there first thing.

He hadn't made the cabin his first stop. He had stopped at a roadside motel, a lonely thing that was located miles to the west, on the border of the county. He had already had a prior engagement with a prostitute there. A monthly engagement that he had to keep or lose his spot.

She was a nobody. Just a girl he had met one night in the next county over, at a bar. But he liked her. And it was his downtime. Still, Major wouldn't be happy with his sense of priority.

So now what was he going to do?

He had messed up.

He had messed up because there was a truck driving to the cabin. And not just any truck. It was Hellbent's marshal. And she wasn't alone.

There was a trooper in the truck with her.

He put the field glasses back into his saddlebag. They sank down to the bottom from the weight. He moved them aside and drew out a Smith and Wesson 500 Magnum, loaded with Magnum rounds. It was an X-frame silver handgun, more commonly known as a hand cannon, and even more widely recognized as Dirty Harry's hand cannon.

Even though the weapon was fully loaded, Major's man liked the sight of the back of the Magnum rounds in the cylinder, so he popped it out and checked it and spun it, and he flicked the cylinder back into the weapon. The next bullet was loaded and ready to fire.

None of it had been necessary, but the act of doing it put a smile on his face. It was up there with pumping a shotgun or pulling a trigger. It got his adrenaline up. It got his blood pumping. It got his engine revved.

Like the other eight guys in Major's crew, he was formerly a part of a dangerous military unit in the United States Armed Forces. None of them were from the same unit. None of them was exclusive. Each of them had once served the country they loved.

Each of them had proven himself in battle.

In the Old West, a gunfighter had notches on his belt from his kills. Similarly, they all had their fair share of notches.

Major's guy watched the truck drive cautiously up the track. He saw faraway plumes of dust kick up behind it.

He put the Smith and Wesson back into his saddlebag.

He knew what he had to do. He had messed up. He couldn't beat them back to the cabin. No way. There was one way in and one way out. He couldn't get past them without being seen.

He'd have to kill them. Which wasn't on Major's parameters for them, but it was better them than him.

The only chance he had of avoiding murdering two cops was if they drove right past the cabin without stopping. But what were the chances of that?

They were probably out here searching for the fire from the night before.

Major's guy reared his feet back and turned the motorcycle and drove off, back down the breach of the gully, back to the main road, and then back to the cabin to take care of loose ends.

10

THE TOMBSTONE WAS gothic and hard and cracked and ancient. Widow walked up to the edge of the wrought iron, which stopped short at waist height, not his waist, but the waist height of a normal human being. He stepped over it and moved as close to the grave as he could without stepping on it. He knelt, resting on his back foot. He studied the headstone. It was etched with wicked-looking demons or spirits. He wasn't sure what they were. In the corners, they stood guard like gargoyles. They looked to be out of a different time and a different place, like hieroglyphics from a forgotten part of American history.

The scene made little sense to him. Widow had never been much of an art critic.

The center of the tombstone had nothing but a date. It was 1801.

There was no name. No age. No family link. No indication of the cause of death. No indication of who was buried there. Whoever it was, he or she was important enough to get a grave that was geographically in the center of town.

Widow stood up slowly and took another look at it, in case he was missing something. There was no sign posted anywhere.

No plaque posted on a pole to tell the story. No sign of it being a memorial. No personal effects set up on the gravesite —no sign of visitors. There was nothing showing that the grave was a historical thing or anything to explain its significance.

He looked up and scanned the neighborhood. He saw no one.

He shrugged to himself and stepped back over the wrought-iron fence and walked back to the street. He continued following the barber's general instructions until he was back on the main road and found the diner.

The sign outside called the place Mable's Diner.

The inside was like hundreds of roadside diners that Widow had frequented over the years. Cheap cloth booths. Square tables with four seats. Two waitresses on duty. One young one, one older.

There was a long countertop with stools, all-metal legs, all with red vinyl cushions.

Widow skipped the booths and tables and sat down right at a countertop on a stool. Among a group of lumberjacks, he figured, because they had that look. They were all scarred with rough hands and sandpaper skin on their faces and necks. They were all big guys with tree trunk-sized torsos. They could've all been from the same clan, the same family, like a clan of Nordic Vikings, stopping into the local tavern to recon the place before they marched in with hordes of giants, wielding medieval weapons.

Truckers could have the same look, but these were not truck-ers. There were no trucks parked out on the street—no big rigs. No trailers. Just regular pickups and cars.

Plus, these guys wouldn't know the first thing about assimi-lating into any other culture. They looked like they had lived there all their lives.

It would've shocked Widow to learn that any of them had ever gone anywhere past the New Hampshire state border.

Then he thought maybe they worked at a local sawmill. Surely there were sawmills out here. Were sawmill workers considered lumberjacks? He didn't know the answer.

There were three of them at the counter and four more spread out over two square-top tables. They were all older than him. The closest one was maybe fifteen years older. Maybe ten if you factored in that lumberjacks worked heavy labor jobs that required them to expose their skin to the elements and the sun more than other jobs. Perhaps this aged them faster than most occupations, like ranch hands or commercial fishers. They were guys who spent their daily lives being eroded by nature. This might've been the factor that aged them so much.

Judging by the several missing fingers between them, they worked around dangerous equipment.

The scars on their faces showed they had learned how to handle themselves over the years. They had been in more than one scrap.

The biggest one had a wicked scar across his nose and cheeks. It looked like someone had swiped at his face with a machete and didn't entirely miss the mark.

Widow hated to think about what had happened to the other guy.

An old cliché about books and covers was something that applied to Widow in his everyday life. So, he didn't judge these books by their covers. He smiled and said, "Hello."

He didn't ask if someone was taking up the stool next to the lumberjack. There was no one there. No plates, silverware, or coffee mugs in front of it. So he sat down.

The waitress who worked the counter was the younger one of the two, but both spoke to him. Both were friendly.

The younger one was polite, but something was there right under the surface. She had a cold look in her eyes, like a woman sentenced to a life of servitude.

She had thick brown hair, rolled up tight in a bun. She had arm tattoos, not sleeves, but one was a half sleeve, upper arm.

She wore threaded, handmade rope bracelets with little hearts hanging on them. Neither waitress wore an official uniform. Not like the traditional waitress garb. Their clothing was their own, all except for the same white print aprons and plastic nameplates.

Widow took a peek at her nameplate. He read it out loud.

"Mable?"

"Yeah, that's my name. Don't wear it out."

Widow smiled, said, "You're Mable?"

"Yeah."

"You?"

"Yes. Is there something odd about that?"

"No, ma'am. Just…"

"Just what?"

"I never met a Mable who wasn't old. Is all."

"Well, my name is Mable, and I'm not even thirty yet."

Widow nodded, a little apologetically, a little regretfully.

"You'll forgive me. I'm on the road a lot. Just myself. It can be taxing on the brain."

She looked at him crooked and placed a clean, white coffee mug in front of him.

"Coffee?"

He nodded, and a big grin came across his face, like a trained dog running to the sound of a twenty-five-pound bag of food being shaken.

She twisted and went to a counter behind her and returned with a fresh pot of coffee. She poured it, leaving two fingers on the top for Widow to put cream and sugar.

He noticed it but didn't tell her he wouldn't need the space.

He took a drink from the mug and said, "This is good coffee."

Which it was. Not the best in the world, but as far as roadside diners owned by young entrepreneurs went, it was great.

"This is your place?"

"It was my mother's. She left it to me after she passed on."

"I'm sorry to hear that."

"What, you don't think a young woman can run a business?"

"I meant about your mother."

"I know. I'm just picking on you."

Widow smiled, took another pull of the coffee.

"Actually, my mom died five years ago. I've been running this place ever since."

"You're doing a damn fine job of it too."

"Thanks."

"Ready to order?"

"What's good?"

"The Traditional."

She handed him a menu, which was a two-sided plastic affair with breakfast on one side and lunch and dinner on the other, coffee written on both. He took it and placed it down on the countertop. She pointed at a breakfast called the Traditional.

"Okay. Sounds good."

He said nothing about the grave. Widow stayed there for less than thirty minutes, finished his breakfast, and drank two more cups of coffee for a grand total of three before he asked about the grave.

Mable took his empty plate and asked if there'd be anything else.

Widow said, "What's the story with the grave?"

She stopped and stared at him. Cold eyes turned flush as if someone had just woken her out of her coma.

Suddenly, Widow felt as though he had bridged a gap that should've stayed a gap, as though he had opened a sealed room in someone else's house. He had crossed a line that he had no idea existed.

At first, Mable was quiet. After a long moment, she swallowed, and then she slowly spoke.

"What grave?"

"The one on Willow Street?"

The tree-trunk lumberjacks at the countertop stopped drinking their coffees and twisted in their seats and stared at him too. The four at the tables all did the same. They stopped and looked up. Widow felt it. He didn't have to have sixteen years of Navy SEAL experience to feel it. A mannequin could have felt it. It was obvious.

Everything that the lumberjacks did seemed rehearsed and perfectly timed. It could have been part of some dinosaur instinct, some kind of synced, single-minded organism. Seven tree-trunk dinosaurs all part of the same tribe, all turning to the stranger among them.

At first, Widow stayed staring forward. He looked at Mable; then, he returned the stares. He turned in his seat, looked first at the one lumberjack to his left, and then twisted around and stared at the other two, ignoring the four at the table. They weren't the immediate threat. But he didn't forget them.

The other waitress stepped back to the kitchen door, not going in, but lingering there as if she wanted to be near a back exit in case things went the wrong way.

Mable said, "Sorry, Hon. I don't know what you're talking about."

As she turned, he could've sworn there was a look of hurt in her eyes, as if the grave was a sore subject. He sensed he should've known better than to bring it up.

She took his plate and left a handwritten ticket and walked away.

The lumberjacks stayed where they were, but the big one, with the scar across his face, said, "Maybe it's time for you to be moving on, friend."

"What for?"

They said nothing.

"You asking me to leave town?"

"We're simply pointing out that you have finished your meal, and there's nothing left for you here."

"There's nothing left for me anywhere."

Two of them scratched their heads to that remark.

"Don't worry. I didn't expect that you'd get it."

The big one stood up.

Widow stood first. He was off the stool and standing straight up. He said, "No need to get aggressive here, fellas. I'm leaving now."

Widow waited to see what they would do. And they did nothing. The big one nodded and faced forward. The other two followed suit, like dinosaurs sharing a collective brain.

Widow held the check and stared down at it, checked the math, an old habit, and dug the amount out of his pocket in cash. He left a two-dollar tip. Not the percentage that he usually left. The end of his experience wasn't top notch. Now he was even more interested in the untended grave.

Who was in it?

The waitress was lying to him about the grave. That was obvious. But why were the lumberjacks getting all bent out of shape about it?

He knew when someone was lying to him.

Maybe the unmarked grave was a sore subject for some people in town.

He finished his coffee and moved on.

Outside, Widow thought about catching a ride out of town. He knew from firsthand experience that the bus didn't run through Hellbent, but the thought hit him, anyway. He looked up one side of the street, saw plenty of vehicles and people walking, then he gazed down the other side of the street and saw more of the same.

He went left.

11

ANOTHER FIVE HOURS of blazing fire, and no one would've known that a cabin had ever been in the spot that Bridges and Wagner were now standing. But the rain had put out the fire, not soon enough to leave any forensics behind. They were staring at the only evidence they had.

Wagner stood, staring at the black and gray ash that used to be something. His mouth hung wide open.

"What a terrible way to die."

Bridges said, "It is."

"You think they were cooking meth?"

"Not sure."

Bridges knelt on her haunches. She pulled a stainless-steel ballpoint pen out of a shirt breast pocket, kept the tip retracted, and used the end to brush away flakes of ash around a human hand gently. There was no skin. No finger-nails. Nothing but the almost buried bones of something that was once alive, surrounded by ash and muddy residue from the rain.

"What is it?" Wagner asked.

"Look."

He stepped closer and stopped a foot behind her. He stayed standing and leaned forward, peering over her shoulder.

"What are we looking at?"

"Check it out."

Wagner pulled his Ray-Bans off his face and held them down by his side.

He saw nothing at first, but he kept staring, thinking whatever she was looking at would sink in. And it did. He saw it.

"What is that?"

She moved the pen and nudged it with the tip.

"It's a nail."

Wagner said, "Oh my God!"

"Someone nailed this guy to the wall."

"He was murdered."

Bridges set the tip of the nail back down into the human soot and slowly rose back to her feet.

"We've got to call this in."

"Let's look some more first."

He agreed, and they walked the perimeter. Bridges went out to the tree line and walked north and west around the pile of ash that used to be a hunting cabin.

She heard Wagner call out from the front yard.

"Who did this place belong to, anyway?"

"It belonged to Neelan."

"Who's that?"

"He's an old guy who runs a hunting company in town. He sells hunting gear, weapons, stuff like that."

"So, what? He gets hunters coming into his shop for supplies, and then he talks them into renting a cabin out here?"

"Yeah, that's exactly what he does."

"Smart."

"He calls it Sporting Synergy."

"Cool term."

"No, I mean, that's the name of his store. Sporting Synergy Hunting."

Wagner walked farther away from the pile of ash to the very last sign of it and started from there, walking back.

Bridges gazed from ash back out to the forest, like she was comparing something.

Wagner moved slowly, staring at the black dust until he saw something.

He called out, "Bridges."

"Yeah? Got something?"

"Take a look."

Bridges left the tree line and walked over to where Wagner stood. She stopped and stared in horror.

"Shit," she muttered.

They were staring at two more human-shaped piles of ash.

"What the hell happened here?" Wagner said, a rhetorical question.

But Bridges answered it anyway.

"Looks like they were tortured."

They stood there for a long minute until Wagner rocked back on his feet from a gust of wind and said again, "We'd better call this in."

"Who you going to call?"

"My CO, for one thing."

"He'll call the FBI."

"Well, we can't do anything."

"True."

Wagner took a cell phone out of his left pocket and stared at the screen.

"You won't get a signal. Not out here."

"What about you?"

"Are you kidding? No phone will work out here."

Discouragement came over his face.

"We'd better get back then. Whoever did this is probably still in town."

Bridges turned and led him back to the truck.

At the truck, Wagner hopped into the passenger side and stared at a CB police radio.

"That thing work?"

She was already picking it up, preparing to use it.

"It works."

"Good, you can call it in."

"There's one problem."

"What?"

"There's no one to call it in to."

"Right. But what about one of your deputies?"

She shrugged.

"You mean my volunteer deputy? Singular. He's not going to be there. Right now, he's on call. But I'm going to try."

She clicked the button and said, "Colin. You there?"

No answer.

She paused and tried again, waited. There was nothing but static.

She tossed the receiver down and tried her phone again. This time it worked.

She redialed her deputy and got the answering machine at the office.

* * *

At the end of the road to the cabin's ashes, Major's guy rode his hog up over the rise and then down toward the site. He could see the Marshal's truck in the distance, past the trees, tail end hung out onto the dirt road.

Just then, his radio started buzzing to life.

"Weeks. Come in?" a voice said. He heard it because the radio was in his inner jacket pocket.

Shit, he thought.

He swerved over and slowed the hog and stopped.

"Weeks! Damnit, come in!"

It was Attack Dog, his direct superior.

He switched the hog off and pulled the radio out, clicked the button.

"Yeah?"

"Where the hell are you?"

What was he supposed to say? It had been his responsibility to make sure the scene was cleaned up, but he had been too late. Now the cops were there, looking at everything.

"I'm headed to the cabin."

Attack Dog paused and then came on the line.

"You're headed there? You're supposed to have already been there and back!"

Major's guy waited and said, "There's a problem."

"What problem?"

"The cops. They're already there. I've been waiting around, watching them."

"How many?"

"Two."

"The locals?"

"Looks like it."

"I was about to take care of them."

"Take care of them? How?"

"I was going to shoot them both with my Smith and Wesson."

Silence.

"What do you want me to do?"

"Have they called anyone?"

"I don't think so. Phones don't work out here."

"What about the radio? The Marshal's got one in the truck."

Silence again.

"What do you want me to do?"

"Stand by."

Major's guy waited.

After a long minute, Attack Dog came back on the line and said, "Don't let them use that radio."

"Affirmative. What about disposal?"

"Take care of it."

"Another fire?"

"Not necessary. We're not trying to cover up their deaths. Just dump em in a ditch."

"Affirmative."

Major's guy dropped the radio back into his pocket and started the hog. He peeled off the gravel and dirt; the tires kicking up a plume of dust.

He headed to the cabin, back to the scene of the crime.

12

EVENTUALLY, the day passed by like any other end-of-summer day, with a long process of turning to dusk that seemed to last over an hour. The whole progression stretched the shadows on the ground to long, thin versions of their previous selves.

The night sky slowly battled its way to victory, conquering the daylight. Widow was left in early blue darkness until an outside light buzzed to life, followed by the streetlights lining the main drag. The light was an eerie yellow that had it been coming from the sun; the people of Earth would all surely die. The weak yellow light would've meant that the sun was cooling and dimming and that the heat from it could no longer reach Earth.

After he left Mable's Diner, Widow walked to one end of the town and then made a one-eighty and walked to the other, from east to west, almost in a straight line. He stopped for coffee one last time at a small outside café with a walkup service window and park benches out front with patio umbrellas. He ordered an espresso and sat down under the shrinking shadow of a large tree.

Supervised children played in a park across the street. Parents hung out near the gated entrance to the park, socializing with each other. Cars passed. Some drivers would slow and take a gander at Widow like a gorilla in a zoo, and then they moved on.

The grass remained dewy from the hard rain the night before.

Widow finished the espresso and tossed the paper cup into a trashcan. The barista behind the walkup window had told him that no bus ran through Hellbent, but there was an Amtrak. It came through once a day, which he already knew.

He thanked her, and with no choice, he started walking back east to where he had seen rows of motels.

After twenty minutes, Widow stopped on motel row and gazed around. Four obvious choices all right there within walking distance. There were vacancy signs posted everywhere. He had his pick. His first choice was a bed-and-breakfast across the street for no logical reason other than the building was two stories and had recently been painted white with green shutters. A fresh paint job told him that maybe it had newly been renovated.

There was a yard, green and freshly cut. A white picket fence surrounded the yard, squaring off around to the corners of the building.

Widow tried to open the gate, but before he could push it forward, he froze.

He heard the rumble of a diesel engine and the winding of gears and the screech of brakes. He stopped and twisted around and saw one of those big diesel trucks from Mable's parking lot. It was an old model, but the exterior was cleaned and polished to a shine.

The truck stopped on the street, right in its lane. Widow heard the parking brake spring, and both doors opened up. Pairs of heavy legs with heavy boots stepped out.

Two of the lumberjacks from the diner clambered out like aliens out of a crashed saucer. They were having a harder time than most because they were both big guys, overweight in the way an oil drum is overweight.

After the two lumberjacks piled out, a third one came out through the driver's side door.

As he shut the door behind him, Widow saw they were all empty-handed.

They lumbered out and around to the nose of the truck. They formed up in a kite with the leader at the top point, his two sidekicks at either end of what would be the crosspiece, and Widow way down at the bottom.

"How's it going, fellas? I don't need any help to find my way around. I thank you for your interest."

The three dinosaur lumberjacks stayed where they were.

They were all hefty, large men, five years older than Widow in one case, and more than ten in another and one somewhere in the middle.

Widow expected the leader to speak. He did not.

Widow said, "What? You can't think of what to say?"

The leader said nothing.

Widow felt like he was in the twilight zone.

"This is the part where you threaten me for being an outsider, or whatever. You guys always seem to start a conversation that way."

Just then, Widow found out exactly why the three dinosaurs said nothing.

He heard a new sound directly behind him. Coming from the other direction was another big diesel truck.

First, the lights flooded his shadow in front of him. Then the truck stopped, leaving the headlamps on. And the other four large lumberjacks piled out.

Within seconds, Widow was no longer in a pyramid. Now, he was standing at the center of a seven-man diamond formation, not counting himself in the diamond.

Shit, he thought.

13

THE LEAD DINOSAUR lumberjack spoke after all.

He said, "You think you're a funny guy?"

"I've been told so from time to time."

"You come into our town making jokes? Starting trouble?"

One of the other lumberjacks spoke from behind Widow.

He said, "We don't want you here."

Widow was grateful for him speaking out of turn because it gave Widow a reason to twist at the waist and glance back at the four guys behind him. He hated having to worry about a threat from the back. Not an ideal position to be in. But he took it as it was.

He twisted, kept his feet planted where they were, and scanned the four. No weapons in their hands. No gun profiles visible in waistbands. No knives or sharp objects. No blunt tools or clubs or hammers. It meant that they had made some half-assed plan before they found him. In that plan, someone with half a brain, maybe the leader, had ordered them to leave their weapons in their trucks. Surely they had weapons. Lumberjacks had axes and saws and hammers and all kinds of big, heavy tools that would make devastating weapons. No question about it. Country boy lumberjacks had access to and an affinity for weapons and guns.

That no one had any in his possession was a relief to Widow.

"With seven of us, you ain't so funny now."

"I'm not trying to be funny."

"Why you coming into Mable's asking questions that you ain't got no right to be asking?"

"I can ask any questions I damn well please to ask."

"Is that so?"

"That's a fact. Besides, what's so wrong about asking about such a peculiar grave?"

The dinosaur lumberjacks didn't answer that.

Widow had clocked four guys standing behind him almost in an exact diamond formation if he included the three in the front of him, which he did.

Widow said, "So what's the deal, fellas? You here to tuck me in?"

"We're here to offer you a choice."

"What choice is that?"

The leader said, "You can hop in the truck with us and get a ride out of town."

Then he stopped speaking like that was the end of the sentence.

Widow said, "And?"

"And what?"

"A choice requires more than one option to choose from. So far, you've given me one option and nothing else. So, what's the second option?"

"There is no second option. You only got the one."

The wind blew between them and under the carriage of the truck in front of Widow. It carried the smell of rain, distant but maybe headed this way.

Widow could see that the three dinosaur lumberjacks in front of him were squinting their eyes. That's when he realized the headlamps on the truck behind him blinded them, and he was given a slight advantage, which would be welcome because no man's ideal opponent numbers seven. He had handled worse odds, but still not ideal.

"I'll tell you right now. I'm not going anywhere. I'm here to rent a room. I plan to put my head on a soft pillow and get a good night's sleep. None of you are going to take that away from me. Maybe I'll leave tomorrow. And maybe I won't. Maybe I'll look around for a rental. Stay awhile. This is a beautiful town. I think, yeah, that's a great idea."

He nodded and continued, "That's what I'm going to do tomorrow. I'll look for a place to rent."

One of the other dinosaurs spoke out of turn, not the same one from behind him. This time it was the one in the front triangle. It was the one who was maybe five years older than Widow.

He said, "You can't rent here."

"Why's that?"

"Ain't nothing to rent around here. Not for you. You gotta have a job."

Widow kept his head locked forward but flicked to his left, stared at the guy five years older than him.

"What makes you think I don't have a job?"

The guy looked at Widow up and down. He raised one hand to block out the headlamp beams behind Widow. Then he looked over at his nearest buddies.

"You ain't got no job. No way."

"You're right. I don't have employment, not at the moment. But you know what?"

"What?"

"I'll find some tomorrow. I bet that tomorrow, I can get up, find a new house to rent and a job all in the same day."

"You look homeless. Where you gonna get work?"

Homeless? That kind of offended Widow because his clothes were clean and not very old. Plus, he'd just gotten a shave and a haircut that day. Worst of all, the guy telling him he looked homeless was a greasy, sooty-looking lumberjack.

Widow said, "I'll just go down to the local lumber mill and apply there."

The three lumberjacks in front of him looked at each other right after that comment. Widow heard the four behind him make different audible sounds, not quite gasps, but not far from it.

The leader said, "You'd never make it in what we do."

"What makes you say that?"

"You're a big guy and all, but not lumberjack material."

"Explain your reasoning for that."

"You're not qualified."

"What kind of qualifications do you need?"

They paused.

Widow said, "What? You gotta be ugly to be a lumberjack?"

They were quiet.

"You gotta be stupid?"

He paused.

"Both?"

"You gotta be skilled."

"Tell you what. Tomorrow, when I go down there for a job, I'll skip lumberjack and go right to foreman."

"To what?"

"The foreman. Supervisor. Or whatever the hell you guys call him."

They said nothing.

Widow said, "I spent sixteen years in the US Navy. So, the fact is, I'm not unqualified. I'm overqualified. In fact, I'm so overqualified that I bet your boss hears my resume and gives me his job. I'll be bossing you guys around tomorrow. No question."

The leader said, "Not gonna happen."

"You think?"

The five-year-older lumberjack said, "Navy? That's almost as bad as the Air Force."

"How you figure that?"

"Navy's a bunch of queers riding around on boats."

"Oh, yeah?"

"Yeah?"

"You know that from your fantasies?"

"What the hell you talking about?"

"I just assume that you imagined that from your fantasies."

"Fantasies? I don't wanna be in the Navy."

"Don't get offended. Nothing wrong with being gay and liking men."

"What the hell you saying?"

"Just to clear it up with you, though, the Navy is a lot of work and mutual respect. So, don't go to your local recruiter and try to get in thinking it's like it is in your fantasies."

"I ain't no queer."

The other two in the triangle looked over at the guy. Widow wasn't sure, but he figured so were the four behind him.

Two parts of his brain told him to make a move right then. The first was the primitive part. It said now. This was the time. They were all distracted for a moment. The second was pure impatience. It told him it was time, because this was dragging on.

Widow didn't need to listen to the second because he spun on his toes, about-faced the four behind him. The headlamps didn't matter, because he had already mapped their positions in his head.

In an eruption of a prehistoric and primitive powerhouse of violence, Widow exploded at the closest lumberjack to his left, the ten o'clock position.

Widow uppercut the guy right in the chin. He used the momentum of his violent twisting and the power of his left hand to blow the guy right off his feet. He flew up off the ground and came down hard, like a traffic sign blown away by a tornado.

Widow moved straight into the eleven o'clock guy. He didn't pause. He didn't wait. He didn't take a breath.

The ten o'clock guy was hitting the concrete by the time Widow jabbed a right straight into the guy's solar plexus. It was a hard, vicious blow. Six inches north and the lumberjack would've been dead by the time he hit the pavement. But Widow wasn't trying to kill anyone. Not yet.

The eleven o'clock guy didn't hit the pavement at first. Widow walloped him so that he flew back off his feet, and his heavy mass carried him a little down a slope in the road, slamming him into the truck's front grille.

Everyone heard a loud *bang*!

The sound of fat flesh and bone clanked with the cheap metal on the truck's front grille.

The one and three o'clock guys were next, and they both knew it.

The leader and the other two heard the sounds and saw the actions, but the headlamps blocked out most of what was happening. It was as if the drifter knew exactly where to move and where to strike to keep them blinded.

Widow moved into the one o'clock and three o'clock guys at the same time.

He watched as the one o'clock guy tried to swing at him with a right hook. Widow blocked the whole movement with a kick to the balls.

He was blessed with long arms, even longer legs, and a big shoe size.

He didn't kick as hard as he could, but the blow was amplified because the guy ran into it like a car slamming into a battering ram.

Widow could only imagine that the damage was just as devastating.

The one o'clock lumberjack was leaning back on the grille, cupping his groin and moaning like a soprano giving birth.

Widow paid the three down guys no attention. They weren't getting back up. Not right then. He took his time and stood up tall, stretching himself out vertically. His hands fell by his sides, like a grizzly bear standing up on its hind legs.

The three o'clock guy knew he was out of range of his friends. He knew they weren't coming to help him. He knew that for the next moments ahead; he was on his own.

Widow looked down at him, promenaded toward him like he was Bigfoot emerging from the fog, from out of the woods, and here to kill the man chopping down the trees of his home.

Suddenly, the guy got brave, like a shot of adrenaline was needled straight into his veins. He charged at Widow.

Widow let him come and then sidestepped to the right and wound back and flung forward. He shoved the guy with both hands onto the shoulders of the guy to the left and away. The guy came up off his feet and slammed into the front grille of the truck. He hit the passenger side headlamps with his head. A *crack*! roared in the silence.

Widow wasn't sure, at first, if the sound had been the glass from the headlamp shattering or the guy's skull. He figured it might've been a combination of both. The guy was dazed and conscious when he landed on his butt, but he was dizzy, and blood trickled out of his mouth.

That's when Widow was hit with the thought that he'd made a mistake. He took a second to make sure the guy wasn't seriously injured.

That was a mistake because just then, he felt a shattering pain across his upper back, and he heard a loud splintering, crashing sound. He saw splinters of fresh timber crack and dust all around him. A long broken piece of lumber toppled over his shoulder and bounced off the pavement.

Widow collapsed onto his knees like a grand piano dropping out of a four-story window.

His vision became dizzy. His upper back throbbed as if he had been hit with a Louisville Slugger in the back, by a professional baseball player at full force.

His primal brain barked orders at him.

Move! Move!

He instinctively ducked and rolled as far to the left as he could. He was just in time to see the leader of the lumberjacks hammer down a broken board onto the concrete where he had been hunched over.

The lumberjack had slugged him across the back with a long, fresh-looking plank: not a two-by-four but some thinner measurement, which Widow was grateful for. A two-by-four would've hurt a hell of a lot more.

Still, lumberjacks swing axes all day. They have all kinds of overly developed triceps and biceps combined with powerful forearms. Getting hit across the back by a board wielded by one of these guys was no day at the beach. Widow stood up straight. He was slightly dizzy. He was having trouble getting his breathing steady. He reached up and clutched at his chest. At first, he panicked that maybe the vicious blow had ruptured or collapsed a lung, but then his breath came back. The wind had gotten knocked out of him. It was severe enough, but not critical, not life-ending or even game-changing. He had been lucky the guy didn't aim for the back of his head, or worse, his neck.

The back of the neck, at the base of the head, is where all kinds of utilities are housed. It is the utility box of the body.

Widow staggered a bit, trying to step forward. He stayed where he was.

"Not so tough now! Are you?" the lead lumberjack said.

Widow's vision came into focus, and he saw the other two lumberjacks also had weapons now. They must've gone to the back of their truck while he was taking out their friends.

One guy had a huge wrench, and the other one had his work ax, which was a vicious-looking thing. The head on it looked razor sharp.

"You should've taken a beating," the leader said.

"I don't take beatings."

"That's too bad. 'Cause we would've just given you a good one. Probably tossed you in the back of the truck and dumped you outside of town. You' da had a bad headache, some bruises, but you'd be able to walk."

Widow stayed quiet. But he didn't like where this was going.

"Now, we're going to have to dump you at the town clinic. Hope they're open."

"You talk too much," Widow said.

The lead lumberjack tossed the broken board off to the side. He reached back without looking and said, "Ax."

The lumberjack holding the ax stepped up and handed it to him.

That's when Widow saw the guy hadn't been carrying one ax. He had two.

The guy with the wrench charged at Widow first. He ran up the middle of his friends. The guy swung the wrench fast and hard. Another powerful swing. But wrenches are all thick metal and very heavy.

Widow sidestepped right and leaned back on his heels. The wrench narrowly missed him. He felt a gust of wind from the wrench, like ghostly hands grasping at his shirt.

He took advantage of the guy missing and stepped forward into the after-swing. His right hand clamped down on the lumberjack's forearm. His left reared back, fast, and exploded forward. He clocked the guy square in the ear with a colossal left hook. This time he didn't hold back. He hit the guy with deadly intent. Although he wasn't aiming to kill him, now they had lethal weapons. Holding back was out the window as far as Widow was concerned.

The blow rocked the guy's brain in his skull.

Widow kept a solid grip on the guy's forearm and jerked him down to the ground at the same time. The blow sent him toppling over. No problem.

And now Widow had the wrench in his hand.

The two lumberjacks left standing held their axes and stared as Widow stepped back one big step and swung the wrench up over his shoulder and slammed it down on their friend's stomach. A hard, vicious blow.

Widow made it look worse than it was. He aimed to incapacitate, to hurt, to injure, but not to cause internal bleeding or rupture the guy's stomach.

The guy who had had the wrench screamed and puked his guts out right there on the concrete.

"Come on, guys. Just the two of you left."

The last two lumberjacks looked at each other.

Widow could see one of them trembled a bit.

He was not looking forward to two huge guys wielding axes to run at him, but one element of the many mottoes of SEALs is never to show fear. For Widow, that was automatic. He didn't show fear. He didn't run from fear. He ran toward it.

The two remaining lumberjacks finally made a correct tactical decision. They charged him at the same time.

Widow braced his feet apart and held the wrench out like a balancing bar: right hand on the base and left hand near the head.

The lumberjacks raised their axes and charged.

They never got to Widow because right then, they all heard a loud blast that echoed into the night.

14

THE BLAST ECHOED between the trucks and the buildings. Widow knew exactly what the sound was the moment he heard it. He figured that the lumberjacks also recognized the sound. It was universally known.

The sound was a gunshot from a handgun.

The two lumberjacks froze where they stood, axes still in hand. They both spun around fast to see the origin of the gunshot.

Widow peered past them and saw it had been fired up in the air from a Glock 17. Soft smoke plumed around the muzzle.

Standing there in the same outfit Widow saw earlier was the pregnant woman from the train platform.

"Seven on one seems unfair. Don't you boys think?" she asked. She lowered the Glock to just over her belly and pointed it at the leader of the lumberjacks.

"Ma'am, this don't concern you."

"Don't give me that ma'am shit, like you guys're polite gentlemen."

The leader said nothing to that.

"Drop the hatchets."

They looked at each other.

She pointed the Glock at the leader, full out in front of her like a cop catching a perp at gunpoint.

Widow noticed her feet were planted firmly. She kept both eyes open and aimed over the Glock's sights with her right eye. She didn't close one eye. She didn't use her left eye while firing with her right like most amateur shooters do.

She had a lot of practice with firearms.

The leader dropped the ax.

The other guy said, "These are our work axes."

The woman flicked her attention over to him, fast, like someone who did a lot of live drills.

"Drop it, Paul Bunyan."

The lumberjack glanced over at his leader. Widow saw he looked confused. Then he glanced back at the woman and spoke.

"My name's Ryan, ma'am."

"I see we got a Rhodes Scholar here."

"Pardon me, ma'am."

"I told you to cut the ma'am shit. Now drop the weapon."

The guy complied and tossed the ax. He looked over at the leader, who was holding his hands up over his shoulders like you do when you're at gunpoint.

Widow stayed quiet.

The leader said, "What about him?"

"What about him?"

"He still has the wrench."

She walked in closer to them but stayed out of reach in case one of them got it in his head to swipe the Glock out of her hands.

"You morons let one guy kick your ass. And then you let a pregnant woman get the drop on you. So, that wrench belongs to him now. Spoils of war or whatever."

They said nothing to that.

"What now?"

"Now, you scoop up your friends, pile them into a truck, and then get the hell out of here."

They looked at each other and then around at their friends on the ground. Two of them looked pretty bad. The first two guys Widow hit were both awake and holding their heads like they'd been hit in the head with sledgehammers.

"What the hell are you waiting for? Skip to it!"

She moved away from them, stepped toward Widow, but stayed out of his reach as well. She backed up a little behind him to the other lane and watched as the two remaining lumberjacks helped their two friends that were conscious, but dizzy. Another lumberjack came to after the leader shook him. He seemed like he didn't know what day it was. The last two were trickier. Three of the lumberjacks had to lift both of them up, one after the other, and bring them back to the truck's rear. The fourth one was to drop the tailgate, which was about all he could do right then.

Finally, six of the lumberjacks were piled into the truck with one broken headlamp. The leader came back and stopped to speak, but the woman cut him off before he started.

"No. Nope. Nothing to say. Just keep going."

The leader nodded. He never looked at Widow.

Widow stayed there the whole time. He stayed quiet and watched the entire spectacle.

The lumberjack leader piled into his truck and cranked the engine, and the two trucks and seven lumberjacks drove away.

The pregnant woman stepped forward onto the street and stood by him. This time she was in reach.

"You going to keep that wrench?"

Widow looked down at his hands. He was still holding the wrench. He looked up, scanned the street, and saw a pair of large garbage cans. He walked over and tossed it in. Then he walked over to the axes, picked them up, and threw them into the garbage with the wrench.

"What are you doing?"

"Don't want to leave those lying in the street. Could really mess up the undercarriage of someone's car. Or worse, kids could find them and chop off a thumb."

She asked, "You think kids can do that?"

Widow paused a beat and raised his right hand to show it to her. He faced the back of his hand to her and bent his thumb down to look like it was missing.

"Happened to me once."

She stared at the fake stump and then at him.

"How old are you?"

He revealed the thumb and smiled.

"Missing thumbs are always funny."

"Right."

He shrugged.

She reached down with her free hand, and in fast movements, she racked the slide on the Glock, ejected the round in the chamber. It went flying up into the air. She caught it and kept it in hand and then ejected the magazine. She faced the Glock away from both of them, pointed it at the blacktop, and squeezed the trigger. Now the weapon was reset, unable to fire, and safe. Then she handed the magazine over to Widow.

He stared at it, a little confused.

"Can you take that?"

He took it.

She handed him the bullet.

"Would you put that mag back in for me? It's a little tough for me because the mag is almost full."

Widow nodded and thumbed the round in one-handed.

She nodded and said, "You're military."

He handed the magazine to her.

"Not in a long time."

She took the magazine, reinserted it into the Glock, and pulled her jacket back. She took a concealed holster out of an inside pocket, slipped the Glock into it, and put them both back into the inside pocket of her jacket.

Widow asked, "You got a conceal permit?"

"You a cop now?"

"I was."

"So what? You gonna call your buddies to come and bust me?"

"Nope. Just curious."

"Why?"

"Because you seem to know how to handle that thing. Figured you got a conceal and carry permit."

"I do."

"Does New Hampshire allow conceal and carry?"

She shrugged.

"I've got no idea."

"You're not from here?"

"Nope. You neither, I guess."

"What gave me away?"

"The seven lumberjacks that were trying to kill you."

Widow twisted and looked off in the distance where they had driven away.

"I don't think they wanted to kill me. Just get me to run the hell out of Dodge."

"So hospitable."

"Happens more often than you think."

"You piss everyone off you meet?"

Widow looked back down at her and smiled.

"Why do you think I'm all alone?"

She said nothing to that.

"Where're you staying?" she asked.

"Nowhere right now. I was just about to walk into this bed-and-breakfast to see if I could rent a room."

He looked in the direction of the bed-and-breakfast's front door. She followed his gaze and looked at it.

They could both see that the window next to the door had white curtains, and they were whipping around like someone was there, trying to hide behind them.

"I don't think you're going to get a room here."

An old man stuck his head out from behind the curtain.

"Yeah. You're right. What about you? Where're you staying?"

"I'm in the same boat as you. Come on. I saw a motel on the other side of town. We'd better try there."

Widow nodded, and they started walking. She led the way.

"Let me carry your bag for you."

She said, "You don't have to."

"It's no problem."

She passed it to him, and Widow slung it over his shoulder, carried it like he was hauling Santa's sack of toys.

They walked side by side, back through part of town. They wound around trees, past closed daytime shops, past Mable's Diner, past residential sales offices, past a bank, and past a church with a tall spiral steeple like something out of the Civil War era. They walked past the street that led to the road where Widow had seen the lone grave.

Widow introduced himself in name only and asked her name.

"I'm Star. Star Harvard."

"You knew I was military. Are you military?"

"What makes you ask me that? You think I'm butch?"

Widow shook his head.

"No. I think you're the most feminine woman in this whole town."

"So, what makes you ask me that?"

"The Glock."

"Well, Jack Widow, I don't know if you knew this, but every American has the right to bear arms. It's this little thing called the Second Amendment. It's not just military personnel."

"No arguing from me. But it's not just the Glock. It's how you handle it."

"What's strange about the way I handle it?"

"You seem to know what you're doing with it. You checked it properly."

"I shoot a lot."

"It's more than that."

"I was taught gun responsibility."

"I'm not talking about how safe you are with it. I'm talking about how you pointed it at the lumberjacks."

She stopped and looked both ways and pointed at the street across a four-way stop.

"That way, I think."

He followed her across the street.

She asked, "What about the way I pointed it at them. There's only one way to point a gun at someone; muzzle end goes toward the bad guys."

"It wasn't the physical way you held it. It was the fact that you were going to shoot it. If they had provoked you."

"Well, of course, I was going to shoot it. A gun pointed at a target is useless if you don't intend to use it."

"Yeah, but for most people, there's a question in their eyes. For you, I had no question. If you'd pointed at me, I would've feared getting shot."

"And normally, when someone points a gun at you, you're not scared of getting shot?"

"Truthfully, no, I'm hardly ever afraid of getting shot when someone points a gun at me."

She stopped near a wall of an all-night laundromat. Someone came out a glass door to the front, and a bell dinged from above the door.

"Do you have guns pointed at you a lot?"

He smiled.

"You could say that."

She continued, and he followed. She pointed down the street.

"That's a motel I saw earlier when I was price shopping. It looks like it was here before the town. But it's cheap."

"I'm not the queen of England. Cheap will do for me."

After a moment passed, she said, "I was military police."

"Really?"

"Yeah."

"Army?"

"Air Force."

"Security Services."

"Yeah. What branch were you in?"

"Navy."

"Nice. What were you?"

"Most of my time, I was a SEAL."

"Funny."

"Why do you say that?"

"I was just thinking about how it must feel for a big, bad Navy SEAL like you to have your life saved by a chick."

She smiled.

"I've had it saved by many chicks."

"There are women in the SEALs, are there?"

"Not so far. But plenty in uniform."

They entered the motel and saw a young man standing behind the counter, with another one seated on an armchair not far from the counter. The one in the chair appeared to be his friend, hanging out with his buddy while he worked— nothing else to do around here at night for teenagers. Widow knew the predicament well. Decades ago, but still fresh in his memory.

"Got empty rooms?" Harvard asked.

"We do. But..." the kid trailed off and took a long look at Widow. He stared for a good, long minute.

Harvard snapped her fingers at him like she was breaking him out of a hypnotic trance.

"But what?"

"Oh. But we don't have any king-sized beds left. Not for the night."

"You got queens?"

"No. None left."

"Well, I don't need much. What do you have?"

"We got full-size, but only singles. No doubles."

Harvard glanced over at Widow.

"We're not together. We need separate rooms."

"Oh, then yeah, we got empty beds."

"Good. So, ring us up."

Widow smiled and stayed quiet. He looked around the room. The motel was all neutral colors, but mostly some brown and gray hybrid. Wallpaper was everywhere. It was old but clean.

There were fake plants in three corners of the room. At least, he figured they were fake because the office had no windows for sunlight. Just one on the entrance door. Not enough to feed three potted plants.

Widow kept Harvard's carry-on bag in his hand. He didn't want to set it down, not in here.

He walked away from the counter and studied the old photographs on the walls. They were all old, black and whites of different goings-on. At first, he thought they were generic motel photographs, but then he saw they were the town he was in. He saw the lumber mill. Twenty-some lumberjacks and workers were standing out front, posing for a photograph. No one smiled, which made him think it was from a hundred-plus years ago when cameras took fifteen minutes to snap a photo. That's why people weren't smiling in old black and whites. Nobody could hold a smile for fifteen minutes straight, waiting and posing in the same position.

He remembered he'd read that on a bus once from El Paso, Texas, to somewhere. It was in a book about useless historical facts. He liked that stuff.

Harvard walked up behind him.

"Okay. I got us two rooms."

He turned and looked at her. She was holding a single copper-looking key on a ring for him to take. It had a cheap plastic key chain with the room number written on it in Sharpie.

He took it, and she reached up and took her bag from him.

"You paid for mine?"

"Yeah."

"Why?"

"It's that cheap."

"Seriously, why?"

"Come on."

She led him out of the office and started walking around the building. She pointed to his room, which was on the second floor.

"Where's yours?"

"Just below you. I can't do those stairs. I am pregnant, after all."

"You are? You can hardly notice it."

"Funny."

He stayed quiet.

"Thanks for helping me carry the bag."

"Thanks for saving my life."

She looked at him and paused a moment.

"Have breakfast with me in the morning?"

"Sure," he said. "What time?"

"Oh six hundred."

"How long you been out?"

"About a year. Ever since my husband got promoted to captain."

"Where's he?"

This time she paused for a long, long moment.

The wind blew, ringing a pair of chimes in the distance. Dogs barked like they were barking at the wind. Widow heard car traffic on the nearest road.

She finally spoke, but first she made a visible yawn. It was big and obvious, like a signal to Widow, that she was tired.

"Let's talk tomorrow."

Widow nodded and reached out his hand, offered to shake hers.

She slipped her gun hand into his. It looked like two puzzle pieces trying to fit together, but one of them was from a regulation-sized jigsaw puzzle set, and the other was a cinder block of concrete meant as the foundation to a commercial structure.

He squeezed her hand gently.

She squeezed him as hard as she could, as she had probably done her whole career, being that most MPs in every branch were men.

"Good night, Widow."

She had called him by his last name, didn't ask. She was definitely military.

"Good night, Harvard."

They released hands, and he watched her unlock her room and enter and close the door behind her.

He couldn't deny the fact that she was a beautiful woman. Pregnant or not. She had beautiful eyes, a great toned body, a strong will, and a Glock—all the things he liked in a woman.

He knew she belonged to another, and there was no guilt. He was thinking, not acting.

Widow turned and sauntered to a set of black metal stairs that led up to the top floor. He passed a soda machine that hummed and an ice machine that cracked a new round of ice cubes as he stepped onto the bottom rung of the stairs.

He got to his room and closed the door. The inside was like a typical roadside motel, almost to the point of being the same basic room as the motel in the movie Psycho, which caused him to take a peek out the window. There was no old house up on a hill. That's what he had half expected to see. But he could see downtown, the train tracks, car headlights in the foreground, and in the distance, thick trees, rolling hills, and mountains.

Widow returned to the room. He flipped a switch on the nightstand to turn on a lamp. The light was dull and atmospheric. If he had a fog machine, he could have filmed a horror movie scene in the room.

Widow turned the light switch on in the bathroom. It was all white, all basic: sink, shower, tub, and toilet.

He returned to the room, popped his shoes off, set them down against the wall near the door. He took his socks off, his black jeans, white button-down, and a denim jacket with a fabric hoodie. He had bought it all back in New London and washed it once at the home of the girl that he had met in Massachusetts. He looked around the room and thought about what to do with his clothes. There was no closet, no vanity with hangars. There was a dresser with drawers, but he didn't want to fold them up.

He ran the water in the sink and spot-scrubbed his clothes with a bar of soap. He wrung them all out, one at a time, and finally, he hung his jacket off the back of the door, his shirt off the handle, and his jeans off the sink. He dropped the toilet seat and left the socks on the lid.

Widow hopped in the shower and cleaned everything else he owned.

Afterward, he towel-dried and wrapped himself up in the towel. He went over to the bed, turned it down, yanking the sheet out from being tucked in under the mattress because he couldn't sleep in a queen bed with it tucked in. His toes got all mushed down and crumpled over.

He ended up with his feet hanging off the end, which was better than being crammed into the tucked-in sheet.

Widow took off the towel and draped it over an armchair.

He got into bed, killed the lights, and was sound asleep in seconds.

15

Ten miles outside of town and earlier in the day, at the first murmurs of dawn, Attack Dog was the only man in view at the lodge's front porch. He stood there, wearing motorcycle gear like he was a part of a gang, which he was, technically.

He blended in with the occupants of the lodge.

He was alone. He looked at his watch, ten in the morning, but he wasn't looking at the dials on the clock face. He stared onward, past his watch, off into the wilderness around the lonely T-shaped lodge as if he was signaling to someone in the woods, but didn't want to be seen.

Attack Dog stepped to the front door and raised a gloved hand and knocked on it, hard. Six hard fist pounds like a sledgehammer pounding down on the thick wood.

He stepped back and heard muffled voices.

"Who's there?" a female said.

Attack Dog answered. He said a made-up name.

"Sorry to bother you this early in the morning, ma'am. The name's Spencer. John Spencer. I'm having car trouble. Back on the main road. Yours is the first house I came to."

Silence.

"I need to use your phone."

No answer.

"I apologize for the inconvenience."

Another long moment of silence passed. Attack Dog heard more muffled voices. Arguing. Whispering. Contemplating. A serious discussion about the dangers of opening doors for strangers. Then a serious talk about helping someone in need. And the generosity of small-town folk. Then a rebuttal about no one in their little town was that generous. Then the female voice argued for being the better man and setting the proper example.

After this went on for five minutes, bordering on six, with Attack Dog very impatient, the female voice behind the door asked, "Where's your cell phone?"

An excellent question. A wise observation. A scenario that he'd prepared for, naturally. Major had hand-selected him for this mission for more than just his brute force.

Attack Dog said, "Ain't got one, ma'am. If I had one, then I wouldn't be knocking on your door at this time of the morning, now would I?"

He gave her a bit of attitude, a bit of rudeness, which was also a part of the strategy. Be unusually nice to people, and it makes them very suspicious. Be completely rude, and they won't help you out. But be a little of both, and they buy the lie: hook, line, and sinker.

Attack Dog added, "Sorry, ma'am. I'm just frustrated. I walked two miles to get here. I don't believe in cell phones. I'm kinda the outdoors, off-the-grid type. You know what I mean?"

More silence. And more muffled voices.

"I know. Ironic, right? Now's when I need one."

The voices went back and forth some more. Finally, Attack Dog heard a chain on the door and a deadbolt unlocked, and the hinges creaked as the occupants opened the door.

Standing there in the doorway was an older couple and their two sons, maybe. They looked just like them. The sons stood behind them.

The sons were huge, scrappy guys. They were also part of a motorcycle gang. That was obvious. They were all tattooed up and had plenty of upper body strength between them, but not in the midsection. That had gone long ago. They both had long beards.

Attack Dog had expected to wake up the whole house this early in the morning, but the parents seemed to have already been awake. The mom was a tiny thing, with long gray hair pulled back. She was already wearing tennis shoes and casual clothing, like she was going out early. The father looked like he was once big, like his sons, but now he was old and frail. He was not in shoes but was dressed and wearing house slippers.

Both sons hadn't been awakened either; they were still fully dressed minus shoes. But that was only because they hadn't been to sleep yet. They might've rolled in right before Attack Dog knocked on their door. He must've just missed them on the road, which was a good thing because it would've all gone haywire.

The parents stared at Attack Dog up and down, both in separate orders. The sons didn't look him up and down. They both approached the open doorway slowly, with caution in each step.

Attack Dog stayed where he was.

The female said, "We can't allow you to be stranded out there on the road. The wilderness here is big. You could face real dangers."

"That's mighty kind of you, ma'am."

She stepped forward and pushed on a screen door installed decades earlier. It creaked like an old man plagued with agonizing arthritis.

Attack Dog looked at the open door and at the elderly people like he was pondering their invitation.

"Actually, ma'am, I'd like to use your phone out here. My boots are filthy, and I'm afraid I've been smoking."

He pulled a pack of cigarettes out of his jacket pocket and showed it to her.

 "Don't want to stink up your home. I promise to be quick. I'm gonna make a call to my buddy in town, and then I'll be on my way."

"Nonsense. Come in. Bill smokes anyway."

She looked at her husband, and he smiled.

Attack Dog's orders were to get them to step out, which would've made his job easier, but in the field, tactics change. And you have to change with them.

He smiled, put the pack of smokes back in his pocket, and entered.

The wife walked ahead of him and turned a corner to a kitchen. The husband stayed next to his side, and the sons kept a ten-foot distance from him.

"Come on in," the wife said.

Bill said, "Dorothy, get him a cup of coffee."

"Of course. You take it black?"

Bill pointed out a round kitchen table made of thick wood. It'd probably survive gunshots, Attack Dog thought. It could definitely survive nine-millimeter rounds.

Attack Dog took a seat on the outer side of the table, facing toward the kitchen. Dorothy poured him a cup of coffee from a freshly brewed pot and gave it to him. He took it but didn't drink. He set it on the table.

The sons moved in closer, and the father sat in the seat across the table by the back wall.

Dorothy came over with an old flip phone she pulled out of her purse.

"You can use my phone."

"Thanks."

Attack Dog took it and set it on the table in front of him.

"You going to make your call?" one son asked.

"In a moment."

Attack Dog smiled.

"Gonna rest my feet for a second. Been walking five miles just to find you guys."

The younger son nodded along, but the older one moved in closer. He leaned against the corner of the living room wall, right at the border to the kitchen.

"I thought you only walked two miles?"

Attack Dog grabbed the coffee mug and took a sip.

"That's good coffee."

He smiled at Dorothy.

"It's just a store-bought brand."

"Those are always the best."

The older son hopped off the wall and moved in closer.

"I asked you a question."

"What's that?"

"You heard me. You said you walked two miles, but now you're saying five. Which is it?"

Bill said, "Son, back off."

The older son said nothing to that.

Attack Dog took a big gulp from the coffee mug and set it down. He scooped up the phone and made a call.

"Frank, buddy, I broke down out here."

He gave the person on the other end the road name and miles outside of town, which he said was only four. Then he asked, "How long?"

"Nah. We're all in the kitchen. Back of the house."

The sons looked at each other.

"Okay. See you soon."

Attack Dog hung up the phone but didn't hand it back to Dorothy. He set it on the table instead.

She looked at him like she disapproved, which she did.

"In case he calls back. You know, looking for directions?"

She smiled and nodded.

The younger son moved in closer and dumped himself down on the seat next to his father.

He looked at Attack Dog like something had just dawned on him.

"You a part of a club?"

"A club?"

The younger son stared up at the older one.

Attack Dog noticed that the younger son sat in a position where he was forced to look back and forth between the two.

Smart, he thought.

"Motorcycle club?"

Attack Dog nodded.

"I am."

"Which one?"

"You a part of a club?"

"We're a part of New Hampshire Chapter of Demon Dogs."

Attack Dog said, "Not me. I'm between things right now."

The older brother moved in and looked at Attack Dog's vest. He was studying the patches.

That's when Attack Dog saw that the older brother brandished a .45 1911. The gun was modified and customized with flames and compensators.

Bill said, "Son, what's going on?"

The younger brother ignored his father and said, "If you're between things, they don't let you wear patches. You walk out on a club; then, you're branded for life."

Attack Dog said, "I didn't walk out. Just between things. Long story."

The older one said, "The thing is, you've got patches from more than one club on that vest."

The younger son pointed his finger at Attack Dog from across the table. Bill reached out his hand, put it on his son's forearm.

He whispered, "Not in the house."

"You ain't a part of no gang. What are you doing here?" the younger son said.

Attack Dog smiled.

In a fury of muscle and force, he exploded up out of the seat. He threw the hot coffee and mug at the older son's face.

The coffee swept across his face, and he screamed from the heat. Attack Dog was on his feet. He jerked the 1911 out of the son's hand and flipped it, pointed the muzzle into his chest, and squeezed the trigger twice in rapid succession.

Pop! Pop!

The son toppled back into the wall behind him, banging straight into the drywall and sliding down, crushing the wall.

The younger son was on his feet and ready to jump Attack Dog from behind, but he only made it to his feet.

Before the younger son could get any farther, an explosion echoed out of the trees, and a pair of bay windows and metal dividers splintered and burst and shattered into hundreds of fragmented pieces. A fifty-caliber bullet fired from a Barrett sniper rifle from about a hundred yards away ripped straight through the younger son.

His chest caved inward from the front as if it had suddenly imploded. But the bullet exploded out his left shoulder blade. He went flying off his feet and smashed through the window behind him. The only part of his body that remained inside the house by the time he completely landed was his feet. The rest of him lay outside the house on the cement on the back patio.

He was dead instantly before he hit the ground—no doubt about it.

The bullet kept traveling and eventually embedded into a large tree, violently.

Dorothy's screams echoed after the gunshot finally stopped ringing through the trees and the interior of the house.

Attack Dog pointed the 1911 at Bill, who was frozen in fear. He stared at the muzzle of the gun, watching a plume of smoke that seemed to be the last remnant of the bullet that killed one of his sons. He wasn't wrong.

Attack Dog flicked his wrist and pointed the gun at Dorothy.

"Shut up!" he barked.

She quieted.

"Good. Have a seat."

He backed away and pointed at the seat he had toppled over when he jumped up.

Dorothy cowered as she trotted over to it and picked it up. She turned it to face him and sat down.

"Good," he said coldly, distantly.

Silence filled the air. Both of their sons were dead.

Suddenly, Dorothy's flip phone started buzzing on the table. The noise was deafening in the silence.

"Answer it," Attack Dog ordered.

Dorothy trembled and opened it and put it up to her ear.

"Hello?"

"Is my associate there?"

She moved it from her ear and offered the phone to Attack Dog.

"It's for you."

"Just tell him it's all over now."

She put the phone back to her ear and said, "It's over."

"Good. Ask him if he checked for any guns in the house."

Dorothy looked up at Attack Dog.

"He wants you to check for guns in the house."

Attack Dog nodded and asked, "Bill, where are the rest of your guns?"

Bill shook like a lone, wet leaf in the wind.

Attack Dog repeated the question, louder.

Bill said, "There's a shotgun in the hall closet. I'm not sure about the boys' rooms."

"Are there more in there?"

Bill shrugged and said, "I imagine so."

Attack Dog nodded and said, "Tell him I got them all."

Dorothy talked into the phone again. She was meek and lowly.

The man on the phone hung up, and Dorothy hung up, putting the flip phone back on the tabletop.

Doing so, she accidentally stared at her younger son's feet hanging awkwardly over the windowsill. Broken glass was all over the tabletop and the floor and his chair.

Tears ran down her face.

Fifteen minutes later, there was a hard knock at the door.

Attack Dog answered it.

Major walked in, and so did a couple of his other guys, including a man with a Barrett sniper rifle. The man who'd killed Dorothy's younger son.

Major said, "Hello."

16

THE NEXT MORNING, Widow woke up early because of the sounds of rattling pipes from someone running a shower in another unit. Slivers of sunlight beamed through the window across his face and chest.

He must've been dreaming because the covers had mostly fallen off the bed like he had tossed and turned through the night.

He got out of bed, leaving it unmade. He left the covers draped the way they were and went to the shower to check his clothes. They were dry. His shirt was a little stiff, as if he had starched it, which he didn't.

He left the clothes hanging for a moment and heard the faint noise of spray from the shower below him. It was Harvard. She was up and showering.

He couldn't help but picture it in his mind.

She had said she was a married woman. What was she doing here?

Married or not, pregnant or not, she was an attractive woman, and he was a single man allowed to have his own thoughts. He felt no guilt for taking a moment to picture her naked and wet and in the shower.

He shook off the thought and stared at his reflection in the mirror.

Widow had natural muscle. He always had. Good genetics. It was also amplified because of the lifestyle he lived. A man who drifts from place to place, walking a lot, is a man who will naturally be very fit.

Tattoos covered large pieces of real estate on his torso, arms, and back. Each of them had a meaning to him—all of them from a past life.

He looked at himself for another moment. Then he went through the morning routine of a caveman, his morning routine. He took a whiff of his armpit, then his breath, then determined if his smell was acceptable to society. Here, he had to scrutinize himself to a higher standard because he knew that he'd spend breakfast with Star Harvard.

He passed all the smell tests. His breath was fine, but he realized that he no longer had a toothbrush. He had lost it somewhere between the last place he had it and now.

He'd have to buy a new one.

As he thought about the toothbrush, he saw this motel didn't provide toothpaste, as did finer establishments, which was unfortunate because he could put some paste on his index finger, use it as a temporary toothbrush. It was better than nothing.

The mirror on the wall was just a standard, circular mirror—no medicine cabinet hidden behind it. But under the sink was a two-door cabinet, small and tucked away. He popped it open and saw someone had left a travel-sized bottle of mouthwash. The factory plastic still wrapped it.

He opened it and used it.

At least now, his breath would be good to go.

The shower below him had stopped. So, he got dressed and waited for about ten minutes, then left the room, took his key.

In the parking lot, he walked down to the street and looked around.

He mis-estimated how long Harvard would take to be ready. When he came back closer to their rooms, she was already outside and yelling up to his room.

He walked toward her, and she stopped calling his name.

"I didn't know you were already up."

"I wasn't up that long."

She nodded.

"Come on. Let's get that breakfast."

"Sounds good."

They left the motel and walked back toward downtown.

"Let's avoid a place called Mabel's, though," Widow said.

"Why?"

"Just trust me."

"Sure."

They wound up at a small restaurant, part of a chain that Widow had seen a hundred times all over the world.

Harvard ordered pancakes and more pancakes with "loads of syrup," her words. Widow ordered eggs, bacon, and coffee, with doubles on all of them.

The waitress left and returned with black coffee for him and only orange juice for Harvard.

He said, "You don't drink coffee? I never met someone from the military who didn't before."

"I'm pregnant."

"Are you not supposed to have coffee?"

"I read that caffeine isn't good for the baby."

He nodded and had no idea if that was true or not.

Harvard pulled a smartphone out of her pocket, set it on the tabletop.

"You left the bag in the room."

Her face seemed to lose its morning glow.

"Yeah, I'm staying a few days, I think."

Widow sipped the coffee.

"So, what's going on?"

Harvard was quiet for a long moment.

Widow thought back to her, standing on the train platform. That look of being completely lost on her face. It returned. Same look. He reached out one hand and cupped it over hers. The bottom of his palm scraped the top of her wedding ring.

He said, "You can trust me, Star. What's going on? Why did you want me to come to breakfast with you?"

She moved her face and stared down for a moment.

"You'll think I'm crazy."

"I won't."

She was quiet.

He said, "You saved my life last night. Remember?"

She smiled.

"I'm here looking for my husband."

"Where is he?"

She shrugged.

"Here, someplace."

"You came on your own? I saw you on the train platform yesterday."

"I did."

"Brave woman."

"Not brave. I just care about my family."

Widow drank the rest of his coffee and set the mug aside to signal to the waitress for a refill, which she picked up on because she was there faster than he'd seen Marines climb ropes.

He thanked her, and she moved on to take the order from another table.

"I gotta ask you something obvious. I don't want you to be offended."

"You wanna know if I considered my husband ditched me?"

He shrugged.

"Seems the most common thing to happen."

She looked away briefly, as if she was considering how much to share with Widow.

"My husband's name is Jackson Harvard. Captain Jackson Harvard. He's a captain in the Air Force."

Widow nodded.

"Captain or not, airmen do shameful things sometimes. He's human like the rest of us."

Without showing anger, she said, "No way. He'd never do that to me. Trust me. Something's going on with him."

"How do you know?"

"He's my husband."

Widow nodded.

"Yeah, but how do you know? Every man or woman who's ever been cheated on or abandoned out of the blue, ever, has always had the same gut reaction of 'not me. Never me.'"

Harvard bowed her head and moved her hand away from his. She touched her wedding ring and twirled it on her finger with her right hand.

"He wouldn't do that. Trust me. There's more to it than just being missing."

"Like what?"

She was quiet.

"Tell me. Maybe I can help."

She nodded.

"The last time I spoke to him was a week ago. He calls me every Saturday."

"But?"

"This last one, he didn't call."

"That's why you're worried?

"That's part of it. Let me tell the story."

Widow nodded.

"A month ago, he started a new position—a new assignment. We live in North Dakota. He was stationed at Minot. It's an Air Force base."

Widow nodded.

"I've heard of it but never been there."

"We've been there for the past ten years."

"Are you still in the Air Force?"

"No, I didn't re-up. I had the chance a year ago, but I started a local business, and things took off. So, I didn't go back."

"They would've taken care of you during the pregnancy."

"I know. I was stupid, but we didn't plan to get pregnant."

"You didn't plan it?"

She paused a beat.

"I know what you're implying. That he didn't plan it and now he's ditched me because he doesn't want it. But you're wrong. Just trust me, okay?"

"Okay."

"The thing is that I'm not supposed to have kids."

Widow stayed quiet.

"When I got pregnant, I was doing my business, and it shocked us both. Jackson was ecstatic. He wanted the baby more than I did."

"What's your business?"

"I opened a gun store."

Widow nodded and asked, "Minot's got a population to support that?"

"Oh, sure. There are forty-plus thousand people living there. Besides, people who live in places like North Dakota love guns."

Harvard moved away from her ring finger and laid her palms flat on the tabletop. She had remained sitting up straight during the whole breakfast.

Her perfect posture reminded Widow of a time when his mother used to slap him in the back and order him to sit up straight.

Hunching over will stunt your growth, she'd claim. It was a total lie, but it worked. To this day, he hunched over and then corrected it out of fear of shrinking.

"What does Jackson do on the base?"

"He was in the Ninety-First Missile Wing."

Widow leaned back, thought for a moment.

"That's Global Strike now?"

"Yes. Since we first got there back in 2009."

"Global Strike is nuclear."

"Yes."

"Your husband is involved in the nuclear strike system?"

She nodded.

"What happened next?"

"Two months ago, he got orders."

"Transfer?"

"No. An overseas tour. He told me that since he hadn't been shipped out in years, it was his time. There was no dodging it again. He already deferred a few times in the past. And that's true. We tried to stay together. For me, it was easier because I'm a woman. I played that up and pulled strings to stay where he was."

"That still work?"

"It does."

"How about him?"

"He used the fact that he was a captain and in nuclear strike. Not much use for him overseas. But everyone's gotta do it. We all gotta go overseas sometimes. No getting around it forever."

Widow nodded. He knew how it worked.

"Where did he go?"

"He had orders to go to Iraq."

Widow said nothing.

"So, a month ago, he packed his bags, and I drove him to the airport. And watched him get on a plane."

"And?"

"Then I went home to be pregnant and run my store all at the same time. And it was hard. Now, he's missing. He missed his call to me."

"Did you call his recruiter?"

"I'm way past that now."

"How so?"

"I hired a P.I. He was supposed to meet me here. Yesterday."

"That's why you were looking around on the train platform?"

"Yes."

"What did he find? Where is he?"

"I don't know where he is. He's not answering his phone. But I bet it's because he has better cases."

"Better?"

"Higher paying. I didn't pay him that much money. I think he was helping me more out of pity."

"Okay. So, what did he find? Why are you here?"

Just then, Harvard swallowed hard and took a deep breath.

"I called the recruiter. That's when I hired a P.I. Because…"

She paused.

Widow waited.

"The thing is, Jackson never went overseas. The Air Force says they have no record of him getting orders to go overseas. In fact, the P.I. did a lot of digging. He found that Jackson's been discharged for two months."

17

WIDOW SAT BACK in silence until their food came. They both ate, and stayed quiet. Widow finished first, but sat there drinking his third cup of coffee.

Harvard ate her pancakes like Oliver Twist would if given free rein over a casino buffet. She left no stone unturned. No syrupy pancake left. In the end, she licked the fork clean.

"Don't judge me."

"I'm not. Eat up. I can only imagine what you're going through."

She finished and wiped her face with the paper napkin that the silverware had been wrapped up in.

She crumbled it up into a ball and discarded it on top of her empty plate.

The waitress returned and said, "My goodness. Hon, you want dessert?"

"No. Thanks. Just the check."

"Sir, you want dessert?"

Widow denied the offer and asked for the bill. They sat there in silence until the check was delivered.

The waitress waited as Widow showed her he was paying with cash and handed it to her, plus a five-dollar tip.

She thanked him and pocketed the wad of cash with the bill into an apron pocket. She took his dishes next, left the cup. He was still drinking coffee out of it.

As she turned, he stopped her and asked, "Can I ask you a question about the town?"

"Sure."

"Don't get offended."

"I'll try not to."

"The other day, I saw an unmarked grave on a street. It looked forgotten but was set there like some kind of historical marker. Know anything about it?"

The waitress paused and looked like she was searching her brain for the right answer.

"Sorry, I know nothing about it. Can't say I've ever noticed it before."

She was lying. He knew it.

"Never mind then. I was just curious."

The waitress left.

"What was that about? What grave?" Harvard asked.

Widow took a breath and explained it all to her: the grave, his ride in with a state trooper, the encounter with the local marshal, then how he got into an argument with the lumberjacks, and finally to her.

She said, "That's strange."

He shrugged.

"I guess it's some sort of secret thing that the locals are ashamed of."

She said, "The whole town?"

He shrugged.

"I was born in Mississippi. Plenty of towns down there are ashamed of their Confederate past."

"I thought Mississippi was proud of all that. Don't the people there sport the Rebel flag?"

"Some of them. But most of those who do, don't think it's harmful. I think they don't realize how hurtful it is to the black community."

"Why don't they just abandon it?"

"I don't know. Some of them are just misguided. Others know exactly what it means, and they embrace it."

"Hard to imagine that sort of thing in this day and age."

He shrugged.

"America's a melting pot of people who both hate and love each other all at the same time."

Harvard put both hands on her belly and rubbed it.

"Like a family."

"Okay. Like a big family. Lots of families don't get along that well, but they're bonded forever."

"Can't change your family."

"Guess not," he said.

"What now?"

"I'm going to help you. I was a Navy SEAL. We don't leave a man behind."

She smiled.

"Let's get out of here."

She nodded, and he downed the rest of his coffee in one big gulp.

They stepped out of the restaurant and onto the sidewalk.

"How did this P.I. find out that Jackson's not in the Air Force?"

"I told you. They told him."

"Yeah, but who told him? The recruiter?"

"No. I talked to the recruiter. Shiden talked to his sources in the Department of Defense."

"His sources? Who is he?"

"His name is Matt Shiden. He used to be DIA and was a cop before that. He's good. He's solid."

"You trust him? A lot of these guys might see a desperate woman and a quick buck."

"I trust him. Don't worry."

"You sure?"

"Widow, I was an MP, remember? I checked him out before I hired him. He's good. He found stuff I never would've. Like that Jackson's here somewhere."

"How does he know that? Why here? It's the middle of nowhere."

She shrugged and said, "I guess cellphone. Or some kind of illegal surveillance."

Widow nodded. It was possible. If Harvard had run off or whatever he did, he could be in New Hampshire. It was just as plausible as anywhere at this point.

"We should try calling your guy."

"Shiden."

"Yeah."

"Should we do that now?"

"First, I think we should check in with the marshal. Let her know what's going on. Maybe she knows something."

"Sounds like a plan. But first, we have to rent a car. I can't be on my feet walking from one side of town to the other all day."

Widow nodded.

"How do you feel now?"

"I'm good, but even though this town is small, this county isn't. Have you seen a map of this place?"

Widow shook his head.

"I did—several aerial maps of the terrain. Outside of Hell-bent, it's nothing but nearly a hundred miles of wilderness. Mountains. Lakes. Huge trees. It looks like a rainforest from the sky."

Air Force, Widow thought. Of course, she'd checked out a bird's-eye view of the area.

"How did you get those maps?"

"Internet."

"Right. Stupid question."

She stayed quiet.

He asked, "Where are we going to rent a car?"

"Avis is that way."

She pointed east.

"Let's go."

"Where's the police station?"

"It's farther."

"Let's walk."

They headed east.

18

ON THE WAY TO rent a car, they passed the vape shop. Widow looked in the windows and the glass on the door. The lights were off, and the place was still dark.

Harvard kept walking, but stopped and turned back when she saw Widow was no longer beside her.

"Widow?"

He was standing and staring.

"What time is it?" he asked her.

She took her phone out of her jacket pocket and clicked the button and checked the time.

"It's about eight-thirty."

It was morning, eight-thirty in the morning. Widow stared at the glass, the outside part of the door. He wasn't looking through it. He was staring at the times of operation which were posted right there on the door.

"Widow, what is it?"

"They're supposed to be open now."

"So?"

Widow said nothing.

"Do you need to vape or something?"

"Nothing. Let's go on."

19

THEY RENTED a Jeep wrangler after the guy behind the counter tried to talk them down to a more suitable car for a woman in Harvard's condition, his words. Almost his last words.

Instead of knocking the guy's teeth out, like Widow was expecting Harvard to do, she used the guy's sexism to amplify her desire to get whatever she wanted, and what she wanted was to rent something with four-wheel drive and no modern luxuries.

But it turned out that new Wranglers came with quite a lot of luxuries, more than the older models, that was for damn sure. The one they rented was a four-wheel drive, as requested, and the a/c worked great. The chairs were big and comfy. The dashboard was full of knobs and doodads that did all kinds of stuff that they didn't need.

Harvard had the a/c on full blast, which was virtually freezing Widow out of the vehicle, but he didn't complain. He figured maybe she needed it cold because now she had to endure the body temperatures of two human beings. That meant double the heat being generated.

Widow imagined a planet having another planet, two cores heating a planet, can make it all pretty hot.

"Tell me when to turn," she said.

"Keep along this road."

They were looking for the laundromat marshal station. Widow had only been there the one time and couldn't remember the exact location. He knew the direction.

"For such a small town, there's a lot of streets here," Harvard said.

"There's a lot of emptiness here."

She nodded.

"Can I ask you a question?"

"Shoot," he said.

"Why Hellbent?"

"Why not?"

"I mean, why did you come here? This place isn't on any map. How'd you get here?"

"I hitched rides."

"Why here?"

"I'm doing this whole devil stop thing."

"Devil stop?"

"Yeah."

"Care to explain?"

She took a left, and then a right at a stop sign, didn't stop.

"I started out west in Idaho. I found a beautiful place called Hells Canyon. I stayed the night at a campfire with a Canadian couple. They gave me the idea. They were a fan of horror movies or something."

Harvard stopped again, this time for a school bus, empty, but it had the right of way, passing in the other direction.

"And?"

"I stole the idea from them. They talked about visiting all the Devil Stops in North America. Every year they travel to one. This year it was Hells Canyon. I thought that sounded like as good a reason as any to go somewhere."

"So you visited all these so-called Devil Stops?"

"Just some of them."

"You go to Hell's Kitchen?"

"That's the obvious one. I was there last."

"Hell, Montana?"

"It's not in Montana. It's Hell, Michigan."

"So then somehow you heard of this place?"

"Yep."

They made their way around a circle, and they saw the laundromat.

"Right there."

Harvard stopped, and K-turned like Wagner had the day before and parked on the side street.

"That's weird."

"What?"

"That," Widow said, and he pointed out the windshield at a New Hampshire State Trooper vehicle.

It was Wagner's Dodge Charger.

"That's the car I rode in to get here."

"It's a state trooper car."

"I know."

"Why's he still here?"

"I don't know."

They got out of the Jeep and walked over to the Charger.

Widow put a hand on the hood.

"It's cold."

"He must've stayed the night after you left?"

"I guess. But where's the Marshal?"

"Is she upstairs?"

"Doubtful. Her truck is gone."

"Let's check, anyway."

Widow nodded, and they walked over to the same old fire escape that Bridges had climbed down the day before.

At the top, Widow tried the doorknob. It was locked.

Harvard stepped around him and looked into a window. She used both hands to cup the glass. She peered between them like she was looking through a microscope.

"I don't see anyone."

Widow said, "The lights are on."

"There's a coffee pot on the machine. No steam. The light's off."

"That means nothing. Cops leave coffee in the pot all the time."

"I know. Remember?"

She came back up from the window.

"What now?"

Widow turned and descended the stairs back to the main level. Harvard followed.

At the bottom of the stairs, Widow headed back over to the Charger, and said, "I guess we gotta do the footwork on our own. You got a photo of your husband, right?"

"Of course."

She took her phone out again and sifted through the screens with her fingers and came out with a photo of her husband in dress uniform.

Widow looked at it.

"Captain, huh?"

"I told you that."

"What was his name again?"

"Jackson Harvard."

"You don't have a photograph of him?"

"No."

"In your wallet?"

"Who carries photographs around anymore?"

Widow shrugged and said, "Lots of people."

"Guys, maybe. Men are always behind women to adopt modern technology when it comes out."

"What about video games?"

"You play video games now?"

Widow stayed quiet.

"This is all I got."

"It'll work fine."

"So, what do we do?"

"What time is it now?"

Harvard rechecked her phone.

"Close to nine."

"Wagner told me that Bridges has a volunteer deputy. Let's hang out a bit. See if he shows up to work."

"Wagner? Bridges?"

"Wagner is the Trooper. Bridges is the Marshal."

"Okay. What time you think this deputy gets here?"

"No idea. But anywhere from nine to eleven would seem right to me."

Harvard said, "We wait around for two hours?"

"Just a little past nine."

"What do we do while we wait?"

"I think we need to get in touch with your PI. I need to know how he knows Jackson is here."

"I told you already. He's dodging me."

"Maybe he's not expecting someone to call from a different number."

"You'll get his secretary, and she'll dodge for him."

"I won't mention you or Jackson."

Harvard nodded and said, "Okay. Where do we call from?"

"Stay here. Wait for the deputy. I'll find a payphone."

"You're leaving me?"

"I'm gonna walk around the corner. There's bound to be a phone somewhere."

"Okay. How long will you be?"

"Not long."

The sun must've moved higher in the sky right at that moment because Harvard covered her eyes. Then she reached into her jacket and pulled out a pair of gas station bought sunglasses, no brand logo on them. She slipped them on.

"Widow, thanks for helping me."

"Don't thank me until we find your husband. Or at least get answers to what's going on."

Harvard nodded.

She walked to the Wrangler and popped open the driver's side door and pulled herself up onto the seat.

Widow almost offered to help her, but backed off. If she wanted help, she'd ask for it.

Looking like a ballerina didn't make Harvard delicate, like one would think. She was tough—no doubt about it.

Widow nodded and told her he'd be back, and he walked away, turned the corner.

20

Major slapped his boots up on a dusty stone patio table top outside on a square deck in the backyard. He pulled his cigar out of his pocket, relit it, and puffed a long, ominous drag from it, let the exhale slide slow out of his mouth up into the air.

Everything was coming to fruition., the whole plan. All of it. All of their waiting. The only thing that they needed was the missing airman. They needed him to get into the installation. They needed him for recon intel.

Finding him wouldn't be hard. Or it would. Either way, they were getting in. The plan was going all the way.

Nothing would stop it.

And if they didn't find him, then they'd take the installation by force, which they'd probably have to do.

Attack Dog stepped out and nodded at him. He waited like he was waiting for orders.

"Sit down," Major said. "Enjoy yourself a little. We're almost there."

Attack Dog looked at his watch.

"We only got till noon. That's three hours."

"That's plenty of time. So, relax. Where's Prescott and Allen?"

"In the house."

Major held the cigar in the corner of his mouth and pointed at a road in the distance.

"Good. Send them to the site. Tell Prescott to take his sniper rifle. Tell them to stay back and give us a headcount. We know there's at least two down in the hole."

Major reached into his vest pocket and pulled out the crumpled paper that had the coordinates he'd gotten from the airman the night before. He reached it out to Attack Dog, who took it and looked at it.

"This is the location?"

"Yeah."

"It's just down that road?"

"About six miles. Why you think we took this house?"

Attack Dog shook his head.

"Nothing else on this road, Lareno. Nothing else. This is the perfect spot to sit tight till noon."

"What about the other one?"

"What about him?"

Major took his boots off the table and took the cigar out of his mouth. He stood up, walked to the side of the patio, leaned against a post.

He pointed past the trees to a visible gravel road.

"That's the only way in. Right?"

"Right."

"Then relax. He won't get there. We'll see him."

"We should post the truck there."

Major nodded.

"Of course. A little roadblock. Send Jones over there. Tell him to stay back about two miles from the site."

"Rules of engagement?"

"Tell him to keep his rifle out of sight. Shoot if necessary. Tell him to use his badge."

Lareno nodded.

Major said, "If he spots our guy, tell him to take him alive."

"What if he warns them? Telephone or something?"

"They don't have external communication. No phone. No way of talking to anyone unless he is physically there."

Then Major thought for a moment and spoke more.

"Actually, they have a phone, but it comes directly from the White House. Unless our guy is personal friends with the President, then there's nothing to worry about."

"They can talk when the door opens."

Major pulled his watch up to show it to Attack Dog.

There was a countdown in progress. Big green digital numbers counted down. It counted down to noon, obviously.

"What does that say?"

"Three hours and fifteen minutes."

"Exactly. That's when the hole will open. The only thing we can do is find the other one. And we need to find him, just in case. We may have to kill the ones in the hole. It'd be nice to have someone other than Arnold."

"I thought Arnold is a former Missileer?"

"He is, but this's different. Remember? A new thing? There's a new technology in play."

Lareno nodded.

"So, we should be out looking for the other guy."

Major took an M9 Beretta out of a hip holster concealed behind his vest and jacket. He set it on the tabletop, sat back in the chair, and puffed the cigar.

He nodded.

"You're right. I want a minute to celebrate how far we've come. We're beyond the point of no return, the homestretch.

"But we must find him. Of course. Who's left to look?"

"Me, Arnold, Ethans, Warrens."

"Where's Giles?"

"He hasn't checked in since yesterday."

Major said, "He was dealing with the Marshal?"

"Yeah. I've tried to contact him."

"Damnit!"

"Want me to get over there?"

"No. Send Warrens."

"Alone?"

"Yeah. If he's compromised, I don't want anyone else getting mixed up."

"What if Warrens finds him compromised? Like in handcuffs and all?"

"Tell Warrens to kill him. The Marshal too."

Lareno nodded.

Major ordered, "Send Arnold out to look."

Lareno said nothing.

Major said, "And Lareno."

"Sir?"

"That old bitch got any beer in the fridge?"

"I don't know."

"Send her back here."

Lareno nodded and left for a second. He came back with Dorothy, who struggled to free herself from his massive hands. But she couldn't.

Major grabbed her by the back of her collar.

She screamed out in fear.

"Calm down."

She tried to calm herself, but she kept looking down at her dead son. His body was still slumped over the broken window at the back of the house.

Now she could see the look on his dead face.

"What's your name, darling?"

Dorothy was quiet.

Major jerked her one hard tug on the back of her collar.

"Yes! Yes!"

"What's your name?"

"Dorothy."

"Dorothy?"

She nodded.

"Well, Dorothy, you ain't in Kansas anymore. Get that?"

"Yes."

"Good. Listen up. We killed your boys, which makes you maybe think you got nothing left to lose. But you do."

She squirmed in his grip, so he jerked her again.

"Stop it!" He commanded.

She stopped struggling.

"Good. Now, we can do all sorts of bad things to you and your old man. Believe me. Your boys got off easy compared to the things we can do to you and him."

"What do you want from us?" she cried.

"Dorothy, I'm trying to tell you that."

"Are you guys from the motorcycle club?"

Major laughed.

"What now?"

"Our sons used to be part of a motorcycle club. A gang. Is that you guys? Did they owe you money? We don't have any money."

Major bent down so he could look her square in the eyes.

"What makes you think we are a motorcycle gang?"

"The outfits."

Major looked at his leather vest and the patches on it.

"Oh, this shit? This isn't ours. None of us are in a motorcycle club."

Silence.

"We took these from different gangs, actually. Think we collected them from everywhere between Boston and Houston, Texas. I don't even know what the hell most of these patches mean."

"What? Why?"

"Oh, this is all cover."

"I don't understand."

"Don't you worry about that."

Lareno came back and said, "There's no beer. No alcohol."

Major looked at Dorothy.

"Where's the liquor, Dorothy?"

"We don't keep any in the house."

"Why not? Your husband drinks too much? Is he taking out his pain on you? Does he hit you, Dorothy?"

"No. Bill is a good man. We took it out because of our sons."

Major turned his head and looked down at the dead son again, hanging out of the broken window.

"Oh. I see. So, your boys used to run with a local gang. Then they left the gang. And you and Bill made them stop drinking. Does that about sum it up?"

She nodded.

"What about the gang? Where are they?"

"They left town."

Major nodded.

"We need some supplies, Dorothy."

"We got canned foods here. In the pantry."

"Not those kinds of supplies, Dorothy. We need beer. My boys are gonna deserve some after tonight."

"What's tonight?"

He didn't answer that.

"There's a food market in town. They sell beer."

"Good thinking. Lareno, go into town. Take Ethans with you."

Lareno nodded.

"And take Dorothy."

She stared at Lareno.

"Bring her back in one piece."

Lareno said, "No problem."

"And Dorothy, you try anything, you try to warn anybody, I'll burn Bill alive with this whole damn house. Got it?"

Dorothy nodded, but stayed quiet.

21

IT TOOK Widow fifteen minutes to find a payphone, which surprised him he found it that quickly. Then again, Hellbent was a little behind the times in some ways. And it was with the times in others, like having a Vape shop.

The payphone was outside a pharmacy chain, which was open. The phone was housed in an old half phone booth thing. It had a blue plastic shield wrapped around it and still took a quarter, unlike some places which took thirty-five cents.

Widow lifted the phone out of its cradle, checked it for a dial tone. He put a quarter in and dialed the number that Harvard had given him.

He waited.

She had given him the PI's cell phone number, so he should answer it.

Widow realized he forgot to ask if Shiden was from North Dakota or not, but then he dialed the number and realized that the guy was based out of Chicago. It had to be because the area code to the guy's number was 773.

Chicago was in the Central Time Zone, so the guy should be up and awake at an hour earlier than Widow's time zone.

He waited.

The phone dial tone switched to the purr of a landline ring.

After six rings, a man picked up.

"Matt Shiden, PI."

And he said nothing else.

"Mr. Shiden."

"That's me. Who's this?"

"You don't know me. My name is Commander Jack Widow, US Navy."

Widow figured the guy had been avoiding Harvard. He'd be skittish in talking to a complete stranger over the phone, asking about her case. So, titles might help.

"What can I do for you, Commander?"

"First, let me ask you a question."

"Shoot."

"You know what the NCIS is?"

Shiden was quiet for a moment.

"A TV show?"

"Do you know what it's based on?"

"My mother watches it. I never saw it."

"Do you know what it's based on?"

"Army cops?"

"No. NCIS stands for Naval Criminal Investigative Service."

"So, Navy cops then? Military police."

"Right and wrong."

Silence.

Widow said, "NCIS investigates the Navy and the Marine Corps, but they're not military cops, not like the Army. The NCIS is civilian. They're federal agents. The only military unit like that."

"Impressive. What's this got to do with me?"

"I'm an NCIS agent."

A pause from Shiden, and then he said, "Good for you?"

"You know it's a federal crime to lie to a fed?"

Shiden was quiet again, a long moment this time.

"Shiden?"

"Yeah. I know that."

"Good. I'm not threatening you. Just a friendly reminder."

"Ok."

"Ok. Now, a question."

"Shoot. I'll help as much as I can."

"It's come to our attention that you're working a case about a missing Air Force pilot?"

Widow lied about Jackson Harvard's job description. It sounded better if he wasn't right on the money. More believable.

"No. I was working a missing airman, but he was no pilot."

"Would his name be Harvard?"

Shiden was quiet again.

"Mr. Shiden? I don't have a lot of time. The sooner you assist me, the sooner I can move on to Navy business."

"Sorry, yeah. His name is Jackson Harvard."

"That's him. Do you know what his job title is?"

"He's a missile guy. Works in nuclear missiles. Scary shit like that."

Widow said, "Missileers. They're called Missileers. He works with the LGM-30G Minuteman III. Know what that is?"

"A missile?"

"Right. It's an ICBM, nuclear-tipped. Know what that means?"

"It's a nuke?"

"Right. Intercontinental ballistic missile."

Silence. Both ways. Even though Widow mentioned the ICBM, it caused him to hesitate as well. Like a snake recoiling after it used its venom for the first time. If a venomous snake came with a sense of morality, which they don't.

Shiden said, "What's going on?"

"I can't tell you that. NCIS business."

"What can I do to help you?"

"We understand that you're working for his wife?"

"How did you know that?"

"Patriot Act, Shiden. Patriot Act. We know everything."

"Ok," Shiden said.

Widow heard fear and paranoia in Shiden's voice.

"Answer the question."

"I don't work for her anymore."

"Why's that?"

"Because she doesn't pay enough for me to have this headache."

"What headache?"

"All these feds are calling about Harvard."

Widow paused a beat.

"What feds?"

"You and the other guys."

"Tell me."

"There are these other guys. They called once, right after I was packing to meet Mrs. Harvard in some town in New Hampshire."

"Go back to the beginning, Shiden."

"Like you said, Mrs. Harvard was worried about her husband. He stopped contacting her. She was getting nowhere with the Air Force. The husband was supposed to be overseas."

"And?"

"He wasn't. I confirmed that with the Air Force."

"How?"

"Got my contacts. You don't need their names? Do you? Cause I can't give those out."

"No. I don't need those. Just continue."

Widow didn't hear the next thing Shiden said because an automated voice came on, telling him to put more money on the phone. So, he fished out another quarter and dropped it in.

Shiden said, "He never went overseas. He was sent to New Hampshire. A top-secret thing."

"What top-secret thing?"

"I don't know. I know better than to ask questions about government secrets."

"Did you confirm he's in New Hampshire?"

"Oh yeah. At first, he was calling his wife. Well, he called her once that I saw. He used a cell phone. I had it triangulated. Some town in the middle of nowhere."

"Hellbent?"

"Yeah. That's it. How did you know?"

"Then what happened?"

"Then nothing. Mrs. Harvard was insistent on going along to find him. She wanted me to meet her there. I told her it was crazy. She offered me more money."

"Did you take it?"

"Of course I took it, but it was chump change. No way was I going to stick my neck out for that. Not with government secrets involved. Good thing too, cause now you're telling me this might have something to do with IBMs."

ICBMs? Widow thought, but said nothing.

"Mr. Window?"

Widow, he thought, but no reason to correct him.

"You know Harvard is eight months pregnant?"

Shiden was quiet, and then he said, "Sure. I know."

"You let her go to Hellbent all alone and eight months pregnant. And you took her money."

"I'm… I'm sorry about that."

"Better hope our paths don't cross, Shiden."

"Wait? Are you really NCIS?"

"I am."

"It's not a crime to abandon a client. PIs fire clients all the time."

Widow thought for a moment.

"It's not a crime in the state of Illinois, but it is a federal crime."

"It is?"

"What've you done is called fraud level two. Which isn't as high as one, but comes with a ten-year sentence."

"Oh, no. I can't go to jail over this!"

"I'm sorry, Mr. Shiden. It's my duty to report this to the FBI."

"The FBI?"

"A local agent will get in touch with you later today to tell you where you can turn yourself in at."

"Turn myself in?"

"I guess they can send Chicago PD to pick you up, but that adds extra charges. If they come get you, then it looks like you're trying to run. You know how it is."

Widow heard Shiden gulp over the line.

"Isn't there something we can do? An agreement?"

"Agreement?"

"Yeah."

"You trying to bribe me?

"No. No. What if I give the money back?"

"Give it back?"

"Yeah. She wire transferred it. I can just reverse it."

"Reverse it?"

"Yeah. Like it never happened."

"Well, I suppose that if the money was reversed, it might look like you refused to accept payment. Then there'd be no evidence of Fraud Level Two."

"Ok. I'll do that."

Widow said, "You better do that now. Right when we get off the phone. It probably will make the transfer not even accessible to the FBI, since it was reversed in twenty-four hours."

"It's been forty-eight hours."

"That's what I meant. Forty-eight. You'd better get on it."

"I am. Thank you. Thank you."

Widow hung up the phone.

He waited a moment and then reached into his pocket, pulled out his last quarter. He slipped it into the phone and dialed another phone number from memory.

It rang. He got a desk sergeant somewhere inside the Pentagon. She asked if she could help him and he gave her a name.

"One second," she said and transferred him.

He got another voice.

"Civil Aviation Intelligence. Director's office."

The voice was a female, and she didn't use the entire title of the office. It was the Civil Aviation Intelligence Analysis Center or a division of Air Force Intelligence, which meant nothing to Widow. It was DIA. Under the umbrella of Defense, to a man like Widow, what's the difference.

"This is Jack Widow calling for Lieutenant Colonel Darry Stevens."

A pause, and the voice said, "Hold on a moment."

Which turned into another minute, and Widow fumbled through his pockets for another quarter in case this conversation ran over, which he expected it would.

He had no quarter left.

A voice came on just then—a male voice.

"Who is this?"

"I already stated my name. Who is this?"

"This is Director Bruce Carr. Now, who are you?"

"I'm Jack Widow calling for Darry Stevens. It's an emergency."

"An emergency?"

"Yes."

"Then I suggest you call nine-one-one and not the Pentagon."

"It's urgent. I need to speak to Darry Stevens."

"Darry Stevens is no longer here. This is a civilian position. Stevens was here, but he reenlisted to become a one-star."

"Sorry for the confusion, sir. I needed to speak to him, but you'll do."

"I'll do? Son, this is a secure line. How did you get this number? And they didn't switch you over to me. Don't give me that. The switchboard don't work that way. And you dialed direct."

"I knew the number."

"How?"

"Sir, I'm on a payphone and running out of time."

A pause.

"What's the number?"

"On the phone?"

"Yes."

Widow looked at the phone and found the number and recited it to the guy calling himself Carr.

The timing couldn't have been better because right then, he got a warning from the operator and lost connection.

The phone rang back, and Widow picked it up.

"Hello?"

"So, who are you?"

"I'm Jack Widow. Commander, former SEAL."

"Former SEAL. That's not how you got this number? SEALs are tools, not spies."

"I was NCIS, once upon a time."

"So you know Stevens?"

"I do. Good man."

"I never met him. He's been gone a while."

"That's ok. I'm sure you can help me."

"Not likely, Commander. Since my impression is that you're former military and not current, do you work in law enforcement or something?"

"No, sir. This is a personal matter."

"The DIA doesn't deal in personal matters, Commander."

"It's personal as in a personal favor, but it's also urgent."

"Urgent to you isn't urgent to me."

Widow said, "I don't know about that. I got a feeling that you'll be interested in this case."

"What case?"

"Do you know where I'm calling from?"

"A payphone. You told me."

"Recognize the area code?"

"I don't have time for this, Widow."

"It's New Hampshire."

"So what?"

"Sir, I'm going to give you two pieces of intel. One is another phone number where you can call me back."

"Widow, I'm hanging up on you right now. Don't need another phone number."

"The second intel is a name."

Silence.

Widow asked, "Still there?"

"I am. What's the name?"

"Captain Jackson Harvard."

Silence.

"What's that name supposed to mean to me?"

"Look him up. Call me back on this number," Widow said, and gave him Harvard's cell number.

"I'm hanging up now, Widow."

The phone went dead.

Widow hung up the payphone and walked away, hands in his jacket pockets.

He headed back to Harvard.

22

Widow walked back to the laundromat and the marshal office. This time, there were two people inside the laundromat using the machines. Both customers were women. Both were in their twenties. They were friendly with each other and shared a plastic bowl of quarters, brought from home.

They talked in loud voices, like they were competing to be heard over the rotor blades of a Black Hawk helicopter.

Roommates, Widow figured.

He passed them by and walked around the side street to where he had left Harvard. She wasn't by the Wrangler where he had left her. She wasn't anywhere that he could see down the side street.

He moved in further behind the laundromat and stopped and looked around and saw another vehicle parked there, behind the Wagner's Charger.

It wasn't the weirdest vehicle that he had ever seen, not even in the military world. But it was unique.

It wasn't weird in function. It was obviously a functioning vehicle. It wasn't like an experimental Naval land vehicle or anything like that. But it was weird because of the paint job.

It was an SUV, four-wheel drive with no markings on it to show whether it was marshal or police for Hellbent or any other sign indicating that it was an official vehicle of the county, but it had the strangest custom paint job he'd ever seen.

The SUV was an old model, something that Widow couldn't recognize. Maybe it was a nineteen seventies Ford Bronco or something like that. It was boxy and had big windows.

The paint job comprised bright greens and reds and yellows. Painted on the skin of the SUV, stretching out over the hood, doors, and probably the roof, was a scene on the Thames River in London. On one side was the London Bridge, the other Parliament, and in the center was Big Ben. Hovering over all of it was a zeppelin like the Hindenburg; only this one wasn't on fire.

There were spotlights on the streets below. The beams fired out over the bottom of the massive zeppelin.

Widow recognized it. It was the cover of one of the Led Zeppelin albums. He didn't know the name. Why would he? It was unusual that he knew it was a Led Zeppelin album cover.

He wasn't a fan. He recognized it because the zeppelin was a dead giveaway.

The vehicle had to be the deputy's truck. His personal vehicle, Widow guessed.

He deduced that because he heard voices above him, and he looked up and saw Harvard at the top of the stairs arguing with the guy.

Widow walked up the stairs and met them at the top.

The deputy was a tall guy, as tall as Widow, but he had a good thirty pounds on Widow. It was all fat.

The guy had big, broad shoulders, but a gut the size of a tractor engine.

The guy had his keys in the door, trying to open it, but Harvard was haggling him. He looked annoyed.

Widow heard her going off on him. He must've said something rude to her to set her off.

She had her phone out. She was probably showing the deputy that photo of her husband in dress uniform.

The deputy wore blue jeans, cowboy boots, and a button-down denim shirt with the top three buttons undone like he thought he was some kind of Casanova with the local ladies. And maybe he was.

Widow startled him.

That was obvious because the guy spun around and put a quick hand on his gun, which was holstered on his right hip. Like he was being ambushed or something.

The gun was a .38 police special.

Widow guessed the gun and the holster were both oiled up and ready to draw, but so oily that the deputy was just as likely to throw the gun out of his hand as he was to shoot Widow dead.

Widow didn't throw his hands up. He didn't want to spook the guy any more than he already had. Getting shot by some hillbilly cop wannabe wasn't on his bucket list.

"Relax!" he said.

"Who da hell are you?"

The deputy's keys were still dangling in the lock.

Widow saw Harvard; she had taken a step back as the deputy was grabbing at his .38. She was in the guy's left side blind spot. She had her Glock in hand, drawn and ready to use.

Widow squinted at her, furrowed his brow, and moved his hand down low and slow. She realized. She saw it like she was on his recon team, like they were in the desert. It was a signal telling her to stand down, to put the Glock away.

She picked up on it, loud and clear.

She gave him a nod, with a calm face, calm demeanor. She was a real pro. He wondered how many years she'd been a military cop in the Air Force.

Not bad, he thought.

"Relax," Widow repeated.

"Who are you?" the cop asked again.

"I'm with Bridges."

The deputy stared at him.

"Bull shit!"

"Not true. I rode in with Wagner. Yesterday. I met Bridges."

"You rode in with Wagner?"

Widow nodded and said, "Yesterday."

"Why? You don't look like a trooper?"

"I'm not. He gave me a ride. That's all."

The deputy relaxed, but kept his hand near his gun.

"So what you want?"

"I'm with her. We need to talk to you."

The deputy said, "Like I was telling her, wait a minute. Let me get the shop open. And I'll listen to you."

Widow shrugged.

"Ok."

He moved next to Harvard, and they waited while the deputy opened the door and stepped in and closed the door behind him.

"What do you think?" Harvard asked.

"He's a volunteer."

"He's got a badge."

"I'm sure she has to take what she can get."

"Where's the marshal?"

"No idea. Sleeping in, maybe."

"She's in charge of a whole population on her own, and you think she's sleeping in?"

"No. Not really."

"So, where is she?"

"Maybe he's got an explanation."

Harvard said nothing to that.

Widow stood next to her as they waited. The landing was small, which forced him to stand near her in her personal space. If she had a large personal space, then she wasn't showing any signs that she minded him being in it.

He felt her breathing on his face every time she looked up at him. She was taking long, deep breaths. This went on for a moment until he realized she was taking deep breaths, like a woman in labor.

He asked, "You ok?"

"Fine."

Deep breath.

"Just need to…"

Deep breath.

"Sit down. Those stairs were no fun," she said.

Widow thought for a moment.

"Do you know where their hospital is here?"

"I didn't see one."

"They should have one. No matter what size Hellbent is."

"They do. Surely."

She took another deep breath. This time she slowed it and seemed to breathe normally again.

She said, "Why do you ask?"

"When's that baby due?"

"Relax, he's not due for three weeks."

"Still, don't they come early sometimes?"

"They?"

"It? Whatever."

"It is a he. And no, they rarely come three weeks early."

"I thought that happened."

"It happens, but not very common. If they're healthy. My boy is healthy. Trust me. I wouldn't be out here looking for his father if he wasn't up for the trip."

Widow nodded.

Harvard was a tough woman, which reminded him of his mother for a moment. She had been a tough woman.

Harvard said, "Besides, the doctors back in Minot are great. They didn't make a mistake. He's coming in three weeks. No sooner."

Widow thought of something else.

"Is that why you took the train?"

"What?"

"Why you didn't fly here? You got off the train. I saw you. Is it cause you're pregnant?"

"What is this? Biology class? Sex ed?"

"Just curious. I don't know any other pregnant women."

"Yeah, it's why I took the train."

"Ok."

Just then, the door opened, and the ancient bell dinged above it, and the deputy invited them both in.

Harvard entered first. Widow followed.

The marshal's office was a small two-room thing. There were filing cabinets lines along the walls, an oscillating fan, a bookshelf, and one cluttered desk that Widow guessed Bridges shared with the deputy.

On one wall, there was a table set up with a big CB radio that reminded him of the kind he'd seen in ranger stations out in the wilderness.

It had wires snaking out of it and up the wall, vanishing into the tiled ceiling above. It probably connected to a radio antenna on the roof.

There was a wall of windows behind him.

On the opposite wall, behind the marshal's desk, was a huge map of Hellbent and the whole county. It was detailed.

The deputy said, "My name's Colin Cole."

Colin Cole, Widow thought. Interesting.

Cole said, "What can I do you for?"

"Where's Bridges?"

"I don't know."

"She sleeping in or something?" Harvard asked.

"Jo? Sleeping in? Not likely. She's probably out there some-where. I don't know. She's a grown woman. I'm not her keeper."

Widow said, "Shouldn't you know where she is?"

"I'm not repeating myself. What can I do for you?"

"Guess that's why you're a volunteer," Harvard said.

"Pardon me?"

"Can you call her?" Widow asked.

"I could, but I done tried that."

"You tried? When?"

"All afternoon yesterday."

"She didn't respond all afternoon?"

"No."

"That unusual?"

Cole shrugged and said, "It's not normal, but the woman is the boss. She's entitled not to call me back."

"What about Wagner? Where's he?"

This posed a problem for the deputy. The look on his face turned to one of concern, but only slightly.

"That part is odd. Wagner's car is down there, and you saw him. He rarely stays the night."

A moment of silence passed, and the deputy took out a small pack of gum, which turned out to be nicotine gum.

Widow looked at the wrapper, and he knew the brand. He had used it himself once, to help him quit smoking.

Cole shoveled a stick of gum in his mouth and started smacking it immediately. He didn't offer them any.

Cole shoved the pack back in a pocket somewhere in his jeans and smirked.

He said, "Maybe they spent the night together."

Harvard narrowed her eyes and put her hands on her hips and stared him down.

She said, "Make you jealous?"

"I dislike your tone, little lady."

"Little lady?" she squawked in an automatic response that was amplified by her hormones, Widow figured.

"Best not to piss her off, Deputy Cole."

"Piss her off? This is my station. I'll do whatever I want."

They were getting nowhere. Widow thought it best to cool things down.

He used an old trick. He tried to include the deputy in actual police work.

He said, "Yesterday, Wagner and Bridges told me about new bikers coming into town. They were worried about them. They made it sound like they were here to cause trouble. You know anything about that?"

Cole took his eyes off Harvard.

"Yeah. We've seen some new faces on bikes. Don't know if they're bikers, per se."

"Why you say that?"

"The local gangs have been gone for months."

"Bridges said they might be a part of it."

Cole shook his head.

"I doubt it. That gang ain't coming back here. No money for them. They moved on. Only two of them losers left."

"Two left?"

"Just a couple of local brothers. Nothing to worry about. Besides, they're all straight now. Got some nice folks. We haven't had trouble out of them in months."

Widow nodded. He had met the brothers that Cole spoke of. The Vape shop boys.

"Plus, these new guys were different."

"How so?"

"They rode bikes, sure. But they looked tougher than normal motorcycle gangs."

"Tougher?"

"Yeah. And more professional."

"Professional?"

"Yeah. Some of them, not all of them, but several of them looked like they were professional. They were all bearded and wearing biker gear, but they walked and talked and rode in unison like they were filming a movie."

"A movie?"

"You know how on TV, motorcycle gangs always seem to ride in some kind of fancy formation, the leader in the front, and so on?"

Widow said, "Don't have a TV."

Harvard reached down and grabbed Widow's hand and squeezed it like she was saying I'll take over from here.

"Sure. What about it?"

"Real gangs don't ride like that. They're disorganized. There's a hierarchy, sure, but there's no rehearsal on how to ride. You don't have one guy out in front of the rest. The only thing they're worried about isn't hitting another bike with their own."

Harvard asked, "You're saying these guys looked rehearsed?"

"Yeah. Like they were playing parts."

Widow said, "Wagner mentioned a fire yesterday. Out at a cabin."

"Yeah. We got eyewitness reports of smoke and fire. Yesterday. I figured that's what Bridges is doing. Some of those cabins are way out there. Some are two-plus hours and all backroads.

"That's where they are. Probably, went out there and looked around. Maybe they went way out and started asking the neighbors."

"Neighbors?"

"Mountain men, mostly. Lots of them out there. These guys live far apart. Could take them a couple of days to reach everyone. That's probably what they're doing."

"You don't seem concerned?" Harvard asked.

"Bridges can take care of herself. Besides, if she needed me, then she'd have called."

"Can she get service out there?"

"Some places. But not much I can do until she calls."

Harvard remarked, "You're pretty useless."

Cole said nothing. He didn't defend himself.

Widow knew that if he had said that, then he'd probably be in handcuffs.

The power of pregnancy, he thought.

Harvard pulled her phone out and flicked at the screen and came up with that military photo of her husband, again.

She pointed the screen at Cole.

"You seen him?"

Cole leaned in and looked.

"No. Can't say I have."

Harvard slumped her shoulders like she was a little defeated.

Cole said, "But he could be one of those army guys."

"What army guys?"

"There's several of them."

Widow said, "What are you talking about?"

"Some army guys come into town from time to time. They stock up on groceries or grab a bite to eat at Mable's, stuff like that."

"Army guys? Where from?"

Cole shrugged.

"Not sure. Probably one of the installations."

Harvard asked, "What installations?"

"There're all kinds of government property out there."

He turned around and pointed north out into the wilderness.

"There's a road out there that leads to some kind of installation."

Widow stayed quiet.

Harvard said, "What the hell are you talking about? There's a base here?"

"No base. Just a government road. There's a fence around it. Chain-link. The area must be twenty miles."

"What's twenty miles?"

"The area of the fence. You know, like a circle. We get calls from hunters every year, complaining that they can't get past the fence. That's the only reason we know about it."

Widow said, "How do you know the guys are army?"

Cole shrugged.

"Who else would they be?"

Harvard asked, "Could they be Air Force?"

"No way."

"You're sure?"

"Oh yeah. We've seen no planes coming in and out of here. We ain't got no airport. There's certainly no landing strip out there. I don't think. We'd have seen jets if they were Air Force."

Widow and Harvard looked at each other.

Widow asked, "Where's this installation?"

"I only know the road it's on."

"Where?"

Cole turned around and took them over to the map on the wall. He stared at it and put two fat fingers in the center.

"We're here."

He traced his fingers up and north and west.

"There's the road."

He pointed to a tiny, thin vein on the map.

"How far is that from here?" Harvard asked.

Cole shrugged.

"Maybe twenty-five miles. With that Jeep, you can probably get out there in thirty minutes, maybe forty. Lots of dirt roads."

Widow saw something else.

He pointed at the map and asked, "This is the edge of town?"

"Yeah."

"Is that where there's motel row?"

"Motel row?"

"The motels that are full of itinerants?"

"Itinerants?"

"Temporary lumberjacks that come out here and work the mills?"

"Oh yeah. That's all that stay there. Those motels are no questions asked sort of places."

Widow nodded.

"What about the cabin fire? Can you pinpoint the cabin for us?"

Cole shook his head.

Widow asked, "How does this place work?"

"What do you mean?"

"How do people dial nine-one-one?"

"They dial nine-one-one on their phones."

Widow stared another deathly stare at the guy. He was getting annoyed.

Cole sensed it and said, "A dispatcher in the next county gets the call. They call the marshal."

"If they can't get her?"

"Goes to the machine."

"Machine?"

"An answering machine."

Harvard said, "You're kidding?"

"No. It's right there."

Cole pointed behind her at Bridges's desk.

There was paperwork stacked neatly to one side, and more scattered everywhere, and a huge calendar acting as a desktop, where she had scrawled a bunch of things to do on different days of the month.

There was an old computer monitor with wires stringing out the back and vanishing down behind the desk.

And there was a lone, ancient answering machine. It used to be all white, but now was stained yellow from age and wear and probably numerous coffee fingers scraping across the surface.

The machine was ancient. It was the kind that came with a double-sided cassette tape—a miniature one.

A red-light indicator flashed on the front of the machine in quick, rapid beats like a warning light.

There was a digital number in the flash.

The number was one.

One missed call.

Widow said, "You gonna check it?"

"I will."

Harvard said, "When?"

"When I get to it."

Widow didn't step to the guy. He didn't move his hands. He didn't shove the guy. He did nothing that would hold up in a court of law for assault if he was going to a court of law.

What he did was stared at the deputy, a cold stare from the deathly stare he'd given earlier, cranked up to eleven.

He said, "You're a poor excuse for a man with a badge."

"Excuse me?"

"You heard me. You got a missing marshal and trooper, and a pregnant woman telling you that her husband is missing."

Cole stood up tall like he was bowing up to Widow. He walked over to him and got in his face.

He said, "Get out! Both of you!"

Widow stayed quiet.

Harvard shuffled back into Cole's blind spot.

Cole said, "I said, get out! Before I arrest you!"

Widow spoke, but Harvard came out of the blind spot and grabbed Widow's forearm.

"Come on, let's go!"

She pulled him by the arm, and he followed.

23

"WHY DID YOU TAKE ME OUT?" Widow asked.

They stood down by the Jeep.

Harvard smiled at him and said, "Get in."

Widow walked around the hood and took another look at the Led Zeppelin SUV, and frowned at it like it was alive. Then he climbed into the Jeep.

Harvard started the engine and backed out of the side street and started driving.

"Where are we going?"

She reached into her jacket pocket and pulled a small object out. She handed it to Widow.

She said, "To find someplace to play this."

He held the item up. It was the cassette tape from the answering machine. Widow said, "How did you get that?"

"I snatched it while you boys were acting like apes."

Widow smiled at her, and said, "This is impressive."

"I know."

"Problem. Where the hell are we gonna play it? You know what machine will play this?"

"What? A tape recorder. Don't they use the same tape size?"

Widow said, "Where are we gonna get one of those?"

"There's an electronics store. I remember seeing it by the train depot."

So, they drove for fifteen minutes, taking a left and a right and stopping at stop signs, and finally arrived back at the train depot.

Widow saw the barbershop.

There was an electronics store right there on the corner. It had flat-screen TVs in the window, all playing the same program.

They found a parking spot and parked the Jeep and got out.

They walked on the sidewalk, and Widow stopped out front. He said, "Let me borrow your phone."

"Sure."

Harvard handed over the phone.

"Is there a passcode to unlock it?"

"It's 6556."

"Ok. I'll meet you out here."

"Where are you going?"

"I'm going to the barbershop."

"Why? You look like you just got a cut?"

"I did. I'm going to ask if he's seen your husband. This is the only barber in town. If Jackson is here and gets his haircut, this guy will know."

"That's smart," she said. "Ok. See you out here in a minute."

Widow walked along the sidewalk, passing a woman with a baby in a stroller and several other pedestrians, and entered the barbershop.

The barber was alone.

"Hey. You again? You not satisfied with your cut? Want your money back?"

"No. Not at all."

Widow rubbed a hand across the short, clipped sides of his head and smiled.

"So what can I do for you?"

"I have a question to ask."

The barber walked over and moved to one of the empty barber chairs. He sat in it and faced Widow.

"Shoot."

Widow pulled up the phone and the photo and showed it to him.

"Do you know this man?"

The barber looked at the photo—recognition on his face.

"What's it to you?"

"It's important that I find him."

"He owes you money or something?"

"Nope, but he may be in danger."

"What kind of danger?"

Widow ignored that and asked, "Have you seen him?"

"I need to know why you ask? The details. He's one of us."

"One of us?"

Widow stopped looking at the barber and then turned his head and looked around the shop. At the front was a wall covered in photos and awards and one framed American flag.

He turned back and asked, "You military?"

"I was. A lifetime ago."

"Air Force?"

The barber nodded.

"That's right. I was a pilot in the Gulf."

"No shit."

"Yeah."

"I'm Navy."

"Really?"

"Yeah. You can't tell?"

The barber looked him up and down.

"To be honest, no."

"It was a long time ago. I'm out now."

"I like the Navy. Yeah, I know the guy. His name is…" the barber looked away, scratched his chin.

Widow stayed quiet.

"Jack or something," the barber said.

"When's the last time you saw him?"

"They were in here like a month ago."

"He wasn't alone?"

"He comes in with his roommate."

"Roommate?"

"Yeah. Another airman."

"You know what they're doing here?"

The barber shrugged.

"I don't ask questions about top-secret stuff."

"What makes you think it's top-secret?"

He laughed.

"Why else would anyone come way out here?"

Widow asked, "You got an idea about what they do?"

"I don't. But there's like a dozen guys. They're never out in public all at once. I imagine they're here manning something. Probably work in shifts. That's why I only see two of them at a time."

Widow nodded.

"Do you know where they live?"

"I don't. Sorry."

"Is it the motel row?"

The barber didn't ask what that was. He knew. Obviously.

"That's my guess."

"How long have they been here?"

"I only started noticing them about two months ago."

Widow said, "Thanks for your help."

"What kind of trouble he in?"

"I don't know yet."

Widow asked, "Can I ask you another question?"

"Sure."

"What's the deal with the grave?"

"What grave?"

"The unmarked one. On Ignominy Avenue?"

"Why you wanna know?"

"It's curious."

"Not sure I should tell you that."

"Why not?"

"You're an outsider. That's town business. Sorry."

"I got into a lot of trouble over at Mable's about it."

"You didn't ask her about it, did you?"

"Yeah. I did."

The barber shook his head like in disgrace or disapproval.

"You'd better be on your way then."

Widow nodded and turned and told the barber goodbye.

At the door, the barber said, "Mister."

Widow turned and stared.

"That boy may not be Navy, but he's still your family too."

Widow stayed quiet.

The barber said, "Whatever trouble he's in, you help him out, then you come back here, and I'll tell you about that grave."

Widow left and made his way back to the sidewalk, where he expected Harvard to be waiting around for him. But she wasn't there.

24

HARVARD WASN'T THERE because she was waiting at the curb with the Jeep. The engine was running. All the window's down. The a/c was cut off. She looked at home in it, like she belonged.

But her facial expression was something different.

Widow walked up to the driver's side and looked at her. She was holding a tape recorder, brand new. It was right out of the package. There was a torn-open package tossed on the passenger side footwell. There was another one in the cup holder from the batteries.

Widow said, "What?"

"You have to hear this."

Widow leaned in and said, "Play it."

Harvard got closer to him, and she put the tape recorder between them and hit rewind first. When the tape reset back to the beginning, she hit play.

Bridges's voice came over the speakers after a beep sound. It was distorted and airy, like she was in a big open field.

"Cole! Answer the damn phone!"

A pause filled with static, and then she spoke again.

"Cole. Call me as soon as you get in. We found three corpses out here. This was no accident. They were executed."

More silence filled the recorder.

Widow heard Wagner in the background.

"Is he there?" Wagner asked.

"I'm leaving a message."

Bridges came back and said, "Cole, there are three bodies out here, burned to a crisp. Two of them were hogtied with barb-wire. One looked like he was stapled to the cabin, or nailed. It's a grisly scene. Someone murdered these guys."

Bridges went silent for a long moment, like she was looking for the words.

There was a sound in the background, distant, like a car passing. It sounded like an engine roar.

Wagner asked, "You hear that?"

Silence again. The sound was gone.

Bridges came back on.

"Call me asap, Cole! These boys were murdered. And it looks like it was the Air Force boys from out on Tucker Road."

Widow looked at Harvard.

"Air Force boys. It doesn't mean that Jackson was one of them."

She had tears in her eyes. Then she put her fingers up to his lips, telling him to keep quiet.

She let the finger hang there, and so did he.

There was more.

Bridges called out, "Wagner!"

"I see him!"

Then there was inaudible yelling and screaming.

Bridges must've slipped her phone into her pocket, left it on.

Widow heard the distinct sound of a motorcycle engine rumbling, like the ones he heard from Bill and Dorothy's sons.

Suddenly, there was a loud *boom*!

Another followed it, and another and another.

"Gunshots," he said.

Harvard nodded.

The phone went dead, and the answering machine beeped and hung up.

"That's it," Harvard said.

"The Air Force guys. Jackson may not be one of them."

"He's dead," she said.

Widow reached in through the open window, grabbed her, and pulled her close. He hugged her tight.

25

AFTER A LONG TIME, Harvard pulled herself together and wiped her tears away. She ended up hanging off the steering wheel of the Jeep.

Widow stayed where he was until finally she came around and asked him to get in.

He offered to drive, but she refused. Said that driving calmed her.

They drove around the town for another twenty minutes, without stopping or without speaking.

Finally, Widow spoke first.

"What do you want to do?"

Harvard breathed in and breathed out.

"I want to kill them. The men who did this to me. The men who killed my husband. I want to burn them all."

"Okay."

She stopped the Jeep, pulled it off the road. A Chevy honked at her and then passed.

"Are you going to help me?"

"Of course."

"I'm not talking about arresting anyone. Do you want to think about it?"

Widow didn't have to think about anything.

"I'm not a cop anymore."

"What do we do with this?"

She showed him the tape recorder.

"Technically, you stole it. It could be painted as obstruction of justice. These guys committed murder."

"I don't care about that."

"Maybe not, but your boy will need his mom."

"Yes. Of course. So, what do we do with it?"

"Give it to me."

She handed it over.

"I'll make sure it gets back to the deputy."

He slipped the recorder into his pocket.

She said, "How are we going to find them?"

"I know where they're going."

"Where?"

"The Air Force installation out there."

Widow pointed northwest.

"You believe there's an installation here?"

"You said it yourself. Jackson is here. He must've been sent out here."

She said nothing.

Widow said, "Besides, I just confirmed he was here."

"How do you know?"

"The barber."

"The barber?"

"Yeah. I asked him if he saw Jackson. Military guys don't go to salons. He's the only barber."

"Some go to salons."

"Not any I know."

"So, what did he say?"

"He knows him. Told me there's several. They work out at the installation. That's got to be it."

She said, "Why did they do this?"

"I'm not sure. Guess we'll have to leave one alive so we can ask him."

"How many are there?"

"Don't know. But I think they're the bikers that Cole talked about. Think they drove into town disguised as bikers. Some kind of cover."

"Why?"

"I think they're after whatever's being hidden at that installation."

She looked down at the radio and then the dashboard and then back at Widow, stared into his eyes.

"So then Jackson didn't lie to me. He did. But I mean, he didn't ditch us."

She patted her belly.

"No. He didn't. He was stationed here. I'd say it's a can't-tell-anyone kind of situation. You told me you're out of the Air Force for a year now?"

"Yeah."

"He couldn't tell you."

Another tear streamed down her face, and she lifted her sleeve up to her nose, wiping it. She sniffled.

"Sure you wanna do this?"

"I'm not sitting out!"

"I didn't suggest that."

"Good, 'cause you're not getting me to."

She paused a beat, and then she said, "Where do we go?"

"We don't know what the enemy looks like. We don't know how many there are. We don't know exactly where they are. And we don't know who they are."

"Sounds like a dream op."

Widow looked out the window.

Harvard said, "We know where they're headed."

Widow said, "We know they've not gotten there yet."

"How?"

"If they've gotten there, then they've already got what they want. I think that whatever they're after won't fit on the back of a bike. We'd probably have seen it on a big truck."

"Not if it was digital."

He paused, stared at her.

She said, "The Air Force has a lot of valuable digital information. If we're assuming that my husband was tortured and killed to get information, it might've been the kind that comes in gigabytes and not metric tons."

"You're right."

"So, what do we do?"

"We go to the installation. Hope we're not too late."

She started the Jeep up, took her foot off the brake. Widow said, "First, take me to the gas station."

Harvard looked at the fuel indicator.

"We don't need gas."

"It's not for gas."

"Why are we going there?"

"We gotta assume these guys are armed."

"Yes."

"Then, I'm going to need firepower."

"Gas stations don't sell guns."

"I won't be buying one."

"What?"

"Go to the gas station. You'll see."

"Okay."

She drove off.

26

AN OLD GREEN truck cruised up to the parking lot of a local market. Lareno was behind the wheel.

Dorothy and Ethans sat in the backseat. Ethans was snug and close to her. He had a big arm hanging around her like a bear hugging its prey.

They'd just loaded the beers into the back of the truck.

Lareno had stayed in the cab while Ethans walked Dorothy into the market, shopped with her, and waited for her to pay for everything. And he watched her carry the cases of beer out to the truck and put them into the back by herself. It was a struggle. It took her longer than he wanted. But in the end, she did as she was told. She smiled at everyone who said good morning to her.

No one asked about Ethans. She figured that they just assumed him to be one of her sons or a cousin or nephew, maybe.

She walked out of the supermarket with her shoulders slumped and a heavy heart. She had seen her sons murdered in front of her, and her last chance to escape, to tell someone, to cry out for help was gone.

She and Bill were as good as dead. She knew they wouldn't let them go. No way. They'd murdered her sons. They were up to no good. They wouldn't leave witnesses.

But what could she do now?

Lareno started the engine, and they drove out of the lot. He double-checked the faces of the pedestrians in the lot to make sure that none of them looked at Dorothy and started questioning who she was with.

No one did.

Just then, Lareno's phone rang.

He picked it up and drove one-handed back through the downtown streets, back to Dorothy's house.

The phone rang again, and he answered it with his free hand.

"What?"

"It's Warrens."

"Yeah? Did you find Giles?"

"I found him. He was at the cabin like Major said, but…"

"But what?"

"He's dead."

"How?"

"It looks like the poor bastard ambushed the cops here."

"Yeah?"

"And there's more than one. There's a trooper here too."

"Yeah?"

"So, they all shot each other. From the looks of it, he got the marshal first, then he and the trooper exchanged fire. Now they're both dead."

Lareno said nothing.

Warrens asked, "What do you want me to do?"

"Leave them. It doesn't matter now."

"Understood. Want me to join Arnold? Look for the other airman?"

"No, get back to the house. We move in soon."

Warrens gave an affirmative and hung up the phone.

Lareno did the same and drove on.

Three turns later, he noticed Dorothy was staring out the window at a Jeep Wrangler up ahead.

He stayed behind them and then turned behind them. Her eyes stayed locked on the car.

Lareno looked in the rearview at Ethans.

"Ethans."

Ethans looked back at him.

"Grab her by the hair. Make her cooperative."

Without a thought, Ethans snatched Dorothy by a handful of hair and slammed her face into the back of the passenger seat.

She cried out and grabbed at her nose and face.

Nothing was broken. Nothing was bleeding, but her face hurt. She was dazed.

"Why?" she called out.

Lareno asked, "Who the hell is that?"

"Who's who?"

"Ethans, again!"

Ethans slammed her head into the back of the seat. This time, her nose ran blood.

"Her nose broken?" Lareno asked.

Ethans jerked her head back and examined her nose.

"No. She's just old."

"Make me ask again, and he'll break it. Then we'll break more."

"Who is that? Why do you keep staring at that Jeep?"

Dorothy pinched at her nose, held her head back. It ached badly. She thought about her sons. Then about Bill, and then about her nose.

She said, "That's Jack Widow."

"Who the hell is Jack Widow?"

"He's nobody. Just a guy we met yesterday."

And then she explained the situation, explained that Widow was stopping by, explained his helping her and Bill with boxes.

At the end, Lareno turned and followed the Jeep.

Ethans asked, "What are you doing?"

"We have to check them out."

"What for?"

"This Jack Widow saw the truck yesterday."

27

"WHERE ARE we going to get a gun at a gas station?" Harvard asked.

"I'll show you when we get there."

They continued back the way Widow had come when Wagner drove him in the day before. Same streets. Some stop signs. Same stores. All of it in reverse.

Harvard was quiet for a short time.

Widow watched the road ahead. He glanced over and saw that shady-looking motel row. Saw where the itinerant lumberjacks had stayed. Probably some hunters too.

The lots were empty. People were off at work, he figured.

Then he noticed Harvard was spending more time staring in the rearview mirror than the road ahead.

"What is it?"

"That truck back there. It doesn't look like it's following us."

"So, what's the problem?"

"It's not looking like it was following us for a few turns already."

Widow looked in the side mirror. He saw it, faint, a little farther back, but closer than it appeared.

He took a quick look back over his shoulder, and he about-faced back to the front.

"What is it?"

"I know that truck."

"Who is it?"

"It belongs to an old couple. They run a store in town."

"Know why they're making such a big deal about not following us?"

"No idea. It's a small town. Maybe they're going to get gas."

"Maybe."

"You don't think so?"

"I think there's one basic cop in town and he's a fool. I think they know that, and so far, they've followed the traffic rules, including following distance like they're on a driving test, and the tester is sitting in the car with them."

Widow was quiet.

"What do I do?"

"Keep going. The gas station is up there. We'll see what they do."

She said nothing and pulled off onto one of the service drives. An enormous truck loaded with fresh-cut timber on the back passed them by.

It shook the Jeep.

Harvard pulled into the further station to see if the old people would follow, and they did.

She pulled up to the back of the station and hit the brake.

"What now?"

"They're still with us," Widow said out loud, but really to himself.

"Yeah."

He looked around through the windshield to the back of the gas station.

"What are we doing, Widow?"

"I planned to commandeer a firearm."

"From where?"

He pointed to the rows of parked trucks.

"There's bound to be one in the back of every one of those cabs."

"You're going to steal one?"

"I was. Desperate times and all."

"What about now? We still need a gun for you."

"Hold on a minute."

He watched the old, green truck in the mirror.

"There are three people in there."

"So?"

"Well, there was an old couple and two sons."

"Maybe the son is riding with the couple?"

"No way. They were hog riders."

She stared at him.

"They rode hogs. Harleys. They didn't strike me as the type to ride in the back of their parents' truck. Plus, one's missing."

"So, now what?"

"Pull to the back of the trucks, like I'm still going to rob one."

"Are you?"

"Don't think I'll need to. Not now."

Harvard did as she was told.

She drove the Jeep forward and around a large tree growing out of a grassy median. Then she vanished behind the trucks.

The old green truck followed.

* * *

AT THE BACK of the parked trucks, Harvard parked quickly and killed the engine, took the key out, and they both hopped out, fast. They shut the doors behind them.

Widow went left, and Harvard went right.

He ran and slammed his back behind the huge tire of a parked rig. The engine in the truck hummed behind him.

Widow bent down and watched the old, green truck's tires under the trailer.

The old truck pulled up behind the Jeep and stopped and parked. He heard the parking brake. He glanced over in the direction that Harvard had run. He saw her shoes under the trailer of another truck.

She had the Glock. Whatever this was, he didn't want it to get to her.

Widow watched and waited.

He watched for a long moment as the truck just sat there.

Finally, the doors opened, and he saw a pair of enormous boots step out of the driver's side, and he saw a woman's feet and legs get out of the passenger side rear, followed by another massive pair of men's boots.

The woman was Dorothy; he figured.

Right then, he knew something was wrong because she was being shoved out in front of the men. The one manhandled her so much that she barely took any steps on her own. It was like watching two large men walk around with a rag-doll.

Widow heard her crying and whimpering.

The three of them stepped out and stopped flat in front of the truck.

That's when things changed for the worse.

One man called out.

"Jack Widow! Come on out! We know you're here!"

28

"Widow, come on out! If you don't come out, I'll gut this bitch right here!"

Widow stayed quiet.

"Tell him!" the voice said.

Dorothy spoke.

"Jack!" she called out. "Jack! They killed my boys!"

"Tell him!" the voice shouted again.

Widow heard the low rumbling of the truck engines around him.

"They're going to kill Bill!"

Widow looked down at his hands. They were powerful, but they were not long-range weapons, and he knew they had to have guns.

Widow stayed quiet.

One second later, he heard Dorothy call out something inaudible, like she had been punched in the stomach, which was precisely what had happened.

He saw the bottom half of her legs buckle.

"Okay!" he called out. "I'm coming out!"

Shit, he thought.

Widow stood straight up, tall, and he threw his hands up in the air. He walked around the back of the trailer.

There were two huge guys, both rugged, both dressed like bikers, but cleaner. They had clean skin and groomed beards. But they weren't wimps. These were professionals from somewhere.

The one who had been driving did all the talking. He was a big, thick guy. He had a sawed-off shotgun in one hand, hanging loose, pointed at the concrete.

"You're Jack Widow?"

"That's right."

"Dorothy tells us you stopped to help her yesterday like a Good Samaritan."

Widow stayed quiet.

The other guy held Dorothy's wrist in one hand and an M9 Beretta in the other. He stood on Dorothy's side, not behind her. He wasn't using her as a human shield, which would've been a grave mistake if Widow had a gun.

"Do you talk, Samaritan?"

"I talk."

"Good. That's good," Lareno said. "Now, where's your friend?"

"I ain't got no friends."

Lareno looked away, tracked his eyes over the parked trailers.

"Where is your friend? Next time you lie, I'm going to shoot her in the kneecaps."

Widow didn't move. He didn't look around.

He said, "She took off. Probably in the gas station calling the cops. Surely, they'll be here soon."

"What cops?"

Widow glanced at the other one, recording his position, working out scenarios in his head.

"The cops are dead."

"You're the ones who killed them?"

"You knew they were dead?"

"Bridges made a phone call while you shot her. She left a recording on a machine."

Lareno shrugged.

"That doesn't matter. True or not. None of this will matter in…"

Lareno looked at his watch. His mouth moved like he was doing quick math.

"Shit, nothing will matter in forty-five minutes."

"What happens in forty-five minutes?"

Lareno grinned and said, "Your worst nightmare. Not that you'll live to see it."

"So tell me. What are you planning?"

"No. I don't think I will. I think we'll blow your head off now."

Lareno raised the sawed-off and aimed at Widow.

He was at a distance of about fifteen feet, maybe closer to twelve than fifteen. A sawed-off could blow his head clean off, but at that distance, it'd more likely blow his head off, along with his neck and part of his chest.

Lareno put his finger on the trigger, squeezed.

Widow took a deep breath. Maybe his last.

29

AFTER HIS NEAR LAST BREATH, Widow called out in what sounded like desperation.

"Wait! Wait! I got a question."

"What?"

"Did you kill Jackson Harvard?"

Lareno asked, "Who?"

"The missileer."

Lareno paused, took his finger pressure off the trigger, and pulled the sawed-off just a little.

"What're you talking about? What missileer?"

"Harvard. Jackson. He's an Air Force captain. Did you kill him? At the cabin?"

"What do you know about him?"

They didn't kill him, Widow thought.

Harvard was still alive.

"Hey! What do you know of him?" Lareno shouted.

"Take me to your boss, and I'll tell you."

Lareno looked at Ethans, who shrugged. Then he looked back at Widow.

"No. I don't think we'll do that. You don't know shit."

Lareno raised the sawed-off again, aimed at Widow again, and squeezed the trigger.

Before he could squeeze it all the way, Harvard fired her Glock from the corner of a trailer to Widow's left, about twenty-five feet away.

Out of caution, Widow took a quick glance at her, which normally he wouldn't, but he was concerned about her pregnancy. She was well-trained. He could see that the only parts of her she left exposed were her arms, hands, and the Glock 17. The rest of her was hidden behind the trailer's edge.

Harvard fired several rounds, all aimed at Lareno.

Widow turned back and leaped to his feet and ran full sprint at Ethans and Dorothy.

He watched as Lareno's chest and face exploded into a bloody mess of red mist and splattering flesh. The sawed-off was flung from his hand and bounced off the ground. He never fired it.

Ethans looked at the source of the Glock fire. He didn't budge or run. Instead, he jerked Dorothy toward him. It turned out he *was* thinking about using her as a cover, which was a good instinct on his part. Dorothy was a good human shield. She could take bullets for him while being easily manageable and light enough to jerk around as he needed.

The mistake was that many people couldn't chew bubblegum and walk at the same time and he was one of these people.

Ethans pulled Dorothy out in front of him, but the time he spent doing that cut right into his return fire time.

He raised his M9 and started aiming at Harvard, but by the time he was staring at her down the sights of the M9, Widow was on top of them both.

Only thinking about saving Harvard and minimizing the damage done to Dorothy; Widow didn't stop. He ran at Ethans and Dorothy full steam.

The moment before his massive bulk arrived at them, he exploded toward them like a power forward at tackle.

He knocked both Ethans and Dorothy off their feet.

She screamed out but rolled over and off Ethans, out of his reach.

Widow was still on his feet.

Ethans rolled away but came up with the M9. He fired it once, but Widow swatted the M9 down and away. Then he came in with a fast right jab, palm wide open; he nailed Ethans right in the neck.

It was hard enough to kill the guy, but it didn't. Ethans tucked his chin down. It absorbed some of the impact.

He came back at Widow with the M9. He swept it down and then used the momentum of being hit in the chin to bounce back and swipe the gun up. He fired again, just missed Widow's stomach.

Widow clamped down on the M9, hard, and jerked it forward, taking it out of Ethans' hand. He lifted his right foot and kicked out at Ethan's kneecap as hard as he could. He heard the bones in Ethans' kneecap bust wide open.

Widow didn't stop there. Instinct. He twisted back and shot the guy in the chest. Once! Twice! Three times!

And once more straight in Ethans' forehead. Blood and brains and lungs exploded out the back of him.

Ethans fell to the ground in the parking lot, dead.

Widow stood over the guy for a quick second. To Harvard, it looked like Widow was thinking of taking a trophy from his kill, like Predator from that eighties movie.

Then he pivoted and walked over to Lareno, who lay on the concrete.

Widow stared down at him, and Lareno stared back at Widow, only with lifeless eyes. He was dead, too.

Widow looked at Dorothy, who was sprawled out on the ground.

He tucked the M9 into the waistband of his pants and went over to her.

"Are you all right?"

"Yes. But I think my nose is broken."

Widow helped her to her feet; then he held her face in the palms of his hands and looked her over.

"It is. Want me to set it?"

"No. No. I'd better go to the hospital."

"Okay."

Her face was a mess of tears and blood, but she was alive.

"Thank you, Jack Widow."

"Don't thank me yet."

"Bill is still alive."

"Where?"

"Our house."

Harvard came over; her Glock was back in her jacket pocket. She and Widow helped Dorothy walk to the truck.

Widow let the tailgate down, and Dorothy sat on it. Her legs dangled off the back. She breathed in and breathed out.

Harvard said, "Take deep breaths."

She helped her by doing it herself.

"In and out."

After a few minutes of this, Dorothy told them all of it. The bikers. Her sons. Bill. And how to get to her house.

Widow and Harvard offered to take her to the hospital, but she begged them to save Bill. They suggested they call the deputy out of a sense of civil norms like that's what normal people do in these situations, but Dorothy shot that suggestion down. She said that Cole was useless.

"Bill can't wait for the State Police." she cried. She grabbed Widow by the arm and pulled at his jacket. Blood trickled off her face and out of her nose and onto his jacket.

She reminded him the bikers had killed her sons. Bill was all she had left.

That's when they heard a siren. Cole was coming. Someone had called him. Probably the attendant had heard gunshots or one trucker.

"We have to go," Harvard said.

Widow nodded, and he hugged Dorothy.

"I promise you. Whoever did this will pay."

He let her go and walked to the Jeep, but he stopped at Lareno's dead body. He bent down.

"Widow! Let's go!" Harvard called from behind the wheel. She cranked the engine and was ready to drive.

Widow scooped up the sawed-off and checked the dead guy's pockets. He found several shells loose and shoveled them into jacket pockets. Then he stood up and stopped and stared at the guy's face.

"Widow!"

"Hold on! Hey, toss me your phone!"

"Widow! We gotta go!"

"Toss me your phone!"

Harvard reached into her pocket, took out her smartphone, and tossed it to him. He caught it, and stuffed the sawed-off in his left armpit and clamped it there. Then he took the phone, unlocked it, and touched the camera button. He paused, waited for the screen to upload, and he aimed the camera at the dead guy. Snapped a quick photo of the guy's face, which wasn't destroyed, but it was better than the other guy.

Next, Widow bent back down, and rolled the dead guy over, pulled his wallet out of his back pocket. It was on a chain. He jerked it free.

He stood up, opened the wallet, took out the guy's ID. It was completely fake but was a better photo than the guy's bloody face. He snapped a photo, then he tossed it onto the dead body and left it. Took Harvard's phone and hopped in the Jeep.

"Drive!" he said.

She hit the gas and spun the wheel all the way. They turned around and accelerated, tearing through the parking lot and hopping over a curb onto the service road.

Harvard took them back down the service drive, and back into Hellbent.

Widow glanced at the same sign he saw posted the day before with the town name on it.

Welcome to Hellbent.

30

THE JEEP BLAZED out of the gas station parking lot just as a man on a motorcycle was turning in. Widow and Harvard didn't notice the biker, and he didn't notice them.

Warrens went over the hump in front of the same gas station. He rode slowly and cautiously, pulling down the hill and turning in under the roof over the pumps. He stopped the bike, left the engine on.

He heard the sirens in the distance and saw the gas station attendant and two customers and several truckers piling out of the station and staring toward the back of the lot, back to the parked trucks and trailers.

Warrens took out his phone, dialed a number, and put it to his ear.

He let it ring and ring and ring. It was Lareno's phone. No answer. Then he hung up and dialed Major.

The phone rang, and Major answered after the first ring.

"What? You find the airman?"

"No. We got a problem."

"What?"

Just then, he saw the old woman whose house they were occupying. She came walking out from behind a trailer. Her face was bloody, but she was okay. She stumbled on for ten yards, until two truckers, running back to see what was happening, caught her.

"Lareno and Ethans are dead."

"What? How?"

"I think some outsiders."

"Can you confirm?"

"No. Cops are coming here now. But I see the old lady. She's alive and not with them."

"Shit!"

"What do you want me to do?"

"Get back here. Now!"

"You got it!"

They hung up the phone.

Major texted Arnold and ordered him to return, which he responded with an affirmative.

31

WIDOW AND HARVARD drove past many of the same stores and shops they'd seen earlier, but Widow pointed at a road leading to a residential area and told her to go that way to avoid Cole, which she did.

They passed the grave he had seen the day before, but he didn't point it out. And they wound up back on the route to Dorothy's house.

Widow took the phone out and redialed the same number from memory that he had called earlier, the Pentagon and Air Force intelligence. He got the same woman as before and asked for the director.

Director Carr came on the line.

"Commander Widow. You're back."

"I am. Did you look me up?"

"I did."

"Did you look up Captain Harvard?"

Harvard looked over from the steering wheel at him.

"I did," Carr said.

"And? I'm guessing that you found some interesting things."

Carr sighed over the phone, then asked, "Is this a private conversation?"

"It is. More or less."

"What does that mean?"

"I'm with Star Harvard now."

"The captain's wife?"

"Yes."

Carr sighed again and said, "Have you found the captain?"

"Negative."

Carr said nothing to that. He said, "I was actually about to call you."

"I figured you were."

"Why do you say that?"

"Because I figured you'd check me out and somehow you'd conclude that I'm the real deal. And that you need to listen to me."

"That's partially true."

"So explain."

"You understand I can't tell you things."

"And?"

"So I called my friend who works over at NCIS. He's in Special Ops."

"Go on."

"He's fairly high ranking. He's an old college buddy. He was my dorm mate for a summer session."

Widow listened.

Carr said, "We used to golf together. He's very competitive."

Harvard took a curve, fast. Widow hung on to the handle on the passenger door, bracing himself.

Carr said, "He's kept that competitive spirit, even though we are both old men now. So what he does now is he brags to me about cases they've cracked or intel they've gathered about rogue terrorists or whatever. Stuff like that. All friendly."

"I'm listening, Carr."

"I asked about you. I mentioned your name. He told me he'd call me back. So, when he finally did, he casually mentioned that he'd never heard of you."

"And?"

"And that means he has heard of you. Or at least he knows something about you, now."

"He told you nothing?"

"No. In fact, he asked me not to call him at work again. He said there's some kind of crackdown over there about interdepartmental rah, rah, rah."

Widow nodded but stayed quiet.

"So, I looked up Harvard, and he's working on a new project. That's about all I can say."

"If you can't say more, then why did you call me back?"

Carr said, "That's all I can speak."

Widow said, "Can you answer my questions?"

"I can say yes, or I can say no. On most things."

"Is Harvard here because of a nuke?"

"Yes. More or less."

"Is there a secret silo here or an installation that is manned and nuclear-capable?"

"More or less."

"Is this nuke off the books?"

"Yes."

Widow gazed up out the window. His eyes looked over the horizon. The sun was high in the sky. He suddenly imagined nuclear fire everywhere.

"Widow, are you there?"

"Carr, you've got a big problem here. There are hostiles on the ground, and Harvard is nowhere to be found."

"Hostiles?"

"It gets worse. We've got three dead airmen here. Missileers, I'd guess."

"Dead! How?"

"Tortured and burned alive!"

Silence fell over the phone.

Finally, Carr asked, "Are you serious?"

"As a heart attack."

Silence again.

Widow said, "Give me your cell number. I've got photos to send you. I killed two of the hostiles. I need to know if you can identify them."

"Of course. Send them to me. I need to get off the phone for now. I'm gonna try to get in contact with the installation."

"Of course. Good thinking. Warn them that the hostiles may already be on their way or watching them."

Carr said nothing to that, but Widow heard him breathing as if he wasn't sure if he should trust Widow or not. Then he hung up.

Widow went into the photos and fumbled around with them for a moment.

Harvard looked over at him.

"Need me to do that for you?"

"Can you do that and drive at the same time?"

"I'm a woman. I can do anything at the same time as driving."

Widow smiled, handed her the phone. She thumbed through the photos, selected them both, and then left it on a text screen with an empty space where the phone number went. She handed the phone back to him.

"Put in the number and press send."

Widow did as instructed and heard a whoosh sound.

He put the phone down on the center console.

Harvard said, "Widow."

He looked at her.

"I think we're being followed again."

Widow twisted in his seat and saw a motorcycle behind them. Not far, but not close.

Behind the motorcycle was an F150. They might've been hostiles; then again, they might not have.

"What do you want me to do?"

"Keep going to the house."

They drove for another five minutes, and then the phone rang, breaking the silence.

Widow picked it up. The number was private.

"Hello?"

"Widow. Carr."

"That was fast."

"Listen, this is very serious."

"I told you that."

"I've dispatched two teams from Pease Air National Guard Base. But it won't reach the installation for thirty minutes."

"Why the urgency? Talk to me?"

"No one's answering at the installation."

"Would they?"

"Absolutely."

The thought of God knows how many hostiles taking over a nuclear missile smack on American soil sent a chill down Widow's spine.

Carr said, "Widow?"

"I'm here."

"The photo you sent is a man named Sgt. Rick Lareno. He was Special Forces and Army for five years, and then he was imprisoned for five years after that. A string of charges. Eventually, he got out with a dishonorable discharge on some sort of early release. He's not alone. He ran with a bad crew. All kinds of jail time and dishonorable discharges."

Widow listened.

"The leader is a guy named Major Mercer."

Widow absorbed the info and stayed focused on the road ahead, keeping one eye on the motorcycle and truck in the side mirror.

"Mercer got into some hot water over a manifesto he wrote. The short version is he's a nihilist. He and his crew want to dismantle the world order. They've all gone offline over the last month. I checked, and no one knows where they are."

"I do. They're here."

"I agree."

"Looks like they came for your missile, Carr."

"No. There's no missile on that site or plutonium or anything like that."

"So, what's the deal?"

"Since the nineteen-seventies, missile silos have never been updated. The tech is ancient, and it's kept that way so it can't be hacked. It's been left ancient and heavy, so it can't be stolen. You follow?"

"I do."

"Hellbent is a prototype, an experimental idea to change that, down the road."

"And?"

"And the installation at Hellbent is all new tech. It's linked to a satellite, which has been linked to the missile silos."

"Which missiles silos?" Widow asked.

Carr was deadly quiet for a long, bumpy moment.

Widow realized either he was reading the intel about the program in Hellbent, or someone who knew it was telling him.

Carr said, "Theoretically, it's all of them, but there are only five operational."

"Which five?"

"We don't know. It's picked at random by an algorithm."

Widow stayed quiet, pictured the sky of nuclear fire again. Everything was on fire. The trees. The skyline. Everything.

Carr said, "Widow."

"I'm here."

"There's one more thing. The missileers are down deep in a silo, below ground as they all are. Their elevator is on a time lock. Meaning that it only operates when their shift is scheduled to end, and the shifts are always different. Like twenty-four hours and forty-eight, etc. The current shift is scheduled to end in less than thirty minutes."

"Meaning what?"

"Meaning that you'd better get your ass over there! Pronto! Those boys are about to end a shift, and that elevator will operate, and the security blast doors at the top of the shaft will open automatically."

Widow paused, waited for more, but the phone went dead.

32

THE JEEP ROCKED on its springs as they sped up and flew around a corner.

Widow said, "Dorothy's house should be right up here."

Harvard took another curve, hard and fast, and then she slowed at a street corner that led down straight in one direction. She turned slightly down a gravel road.

Widow pointed to a longhouse hidden behind trees and shrubs.

"That's her place."

"So, this must be the road to the installation?"

"Must be. Pull over here."

She pulled over. Widow took out the M9 and ejected the magazine and checked the rounds. He had ten in the magazine and one in the chamber.

He did a check on the sawed-off. He was good there but only could fire two rounds before having to reload.

Widow looked at Harvard.

She spoke before he could.

"Don't you dare tell me to wait here! I'm a part of this. You're not putting me out."

"Okay. This is the plan."

Widow took a quick look at the house and the terrain.

"Give me three minutes to get into position in the back. Then you drive up the driveway. Honk your horn."

"Why?"

"Distraction. You've done this before, right?"

"This sounds more like you're leaving me in the Jeep?"

"There's a hostage in there. You distract them. When they come outside, I'll go inside through the back."

"Then what?"

"Whoever comes out that isn't an old man or me, shoot him."

He reached across the center console and squeezed her hand.

She said, "First, it sounded like you were ditching me. Now, it sounds like I'm the bait."

"You wanted to be included."

She sighed.

He said, "Stay safe. Shoot first. Got it?"

"Got it."

Widow ducked out the passenger side door and vanished into the trees and brush on the corner of the lot.

One minute later, he was around the house and at a back privacy fence built around the rear of the house.

Widow had the M9 in his hand, down by his side. He peered through a crack between planks on the fence. He looked around.

No sign of anyone.

Widow walked to the gate and reached over the top, unlatched it from a simple metal hook, and opened it.

He stepped into the backyard and pulled the gate closed behind him, quietly.

He surveyed the backyard. It wasn't deep and had fewer trees than the front. There was an in-ground pool. Leaves littered the top of it. The water was dark, partially covered in shade, and partially just dirty. He ignored it and headed for the patio and the back door of the house and stopped.

On the patio, he saw the son from the day before. Dorothy's son. He was dead.

He hung across a broken window, left there like a displayed body warning off intruders.

Just then, the wind blew hard through the trees. The sounds carried across the yard. The treetops swayed all in the same direction, like they were grasping toward him.

And something in the pool moved like a wave in the water or something swimming in it.

Widow turned and pointed the M9 at a hump in the leaves in the pool that he hadn't noticed before.

He crouched down and waited. He looked back at the house. The backdoor was a pair of sliding glass panels. There were no curtains. Widow could see into the house. He saw no movement.

Then he approached the hump in the leaves on the surface of the pool. As he got closer, he saw what it was.

There was a dead body floating face down in the pool.

Widow edged to the side of the water and bent down. He reached out with his left hand, kept the M9 pointed at the body, and gripped a wet collar.

Red water pooled around the neck.

Widow turned over the body in the pool.

It was Bill, Dorothy's husband. His throat had been cut from ear to ear. He was dead. No question.

Widow sat back on his haunches, stared into the dead eyes.

He felt terrible for Dorothy. She was all alone now.

Widow felt the hairs on his neck stand up, but not out of fear. It was a side effect of feeling his blood boil. He was furious.

This guy, Mercer, and the rest were going to die.

He stood up, tall, and crept over to the slider. He kept the M9 out, ready to shoot first like he'd told Harvard to do.

Then he slid the door open, fast. It was unlocked, as he had suspected. People who lived way out here probably didn't lock their back patio doors too often. What for? Bears don't know how to click the button and slide the door open.

Widow rushed into the house.

Inside, he found everything he expected—old family furniture, sofas, kitchenware, appliances, a family table, and another dead son.

This one was up against the wall on the way to the living room. Looked like he might've been killed first.

Widow stormed the living room, then down a long hallway, checked three bedrooms and two bathrooms, and four closets.

No one was there.

The place was empty.

He walked back to the living room and saw another door off the kitchen. He opened it and found an empty, dark garage with two motorcycles parked in it. The same two he'd seen the brothers riding the day before.

Widow returned to the living room and headed for the front door to open it and walk out to the driveway to rejoin Harvard.

As he grabbed the doorknob, he realized something. She had never honked the horn.

Widow turned the knob and opened the front door and stepped out into view.

He knew immediately why she hadn't honked the horn.

In the driveway, Widow saw Harvard, pregnant and standing out in front of the Jeep's engine block. She had her hands up. They were empty.

Standing next to her was a man who looked familiar, as if Widow had seen him before, but he was sure that they had never met.

The guy was unarmed. The look on his face differed from the others. It looked almost scared.

He was about Harvard's age and a little taller. He had a bruised eye and split lip, as if he had been roughed up within the last hour. Blood trickled from the corner of his lip. It streamed down his lower face to his chin. It wasn't gushing, but it was still wet.

The guy wore tattered clothes, looking like he'd slept in them, a generic flannel and jeans.

Widow noticed something else, something stranger. The guy was barefoot.

Right there in front of Widow, Mercer stared over at the barefoot guy, scaring him with just a look.

The barefoot guy responded by shooting his hands straight up in the air, like Harvard.

Like Harvard.

The barefoot guy was Jackson Harvard. He was alive and standing right there next to his pregnant wife.

Widow's jaw hung for a split second, but he had to shake it off. He had no time to be surprised.

The Harvards shared the same facial expression. They were terrified.

They were terrified because standing behind them were two men, the same two men that Widow had seen following them in an F150 pickup and on another motorcycle.

They were big, like Lareno and his pal. The one on the bike had the same mismatched patches and the same vest and beard. He wore sunglasses covering his eyes. The sun bounced off the lenses like a sniper scope in the distance.

The guy from the F150 was different. He was short and looked more like the man standing next to Harvard with his hands up, like they were cut from the same cloth somehow.

The F150 driver was plain-looking, clean cut, nothing special.

Then there was another man. He was tall and big and had pale skin.

Widow saw no sunglasses on his face but couldn't see his eyes because there were deep-set, making his eye sockets look like manmade arches.

The man's face was long, horse-like. There were two jagged H-shaped scars lacerated across the man's temple, cutting into his sideburns and his eyebrows, leaving white lines of scars instead of hair.

He had a big, thick beard like the others, and the dead ones that maybe he didn't know were dead, Widow hoped.

The man said, "Jack Widow."

Shit, Widow thought.

The guy knew who he was.

33

"JACK WIDOW," the guy in the front, the leader, said.

Widow stayed quiet.

"You're the one causing me trouble."

"Guess so."

"Do you know who I am?"

Widow looked him up and down. The M9 was still in his hand, but pointed at the ground.

Widow stood in the doorway. He thought about ducking back into the house. He could do that. But then they'd threaten to kill Harvard if he didn't come out. He knew this game.

"You must be Mercer?"

"You know me," Mercer said and twisted at the waist and looked back at the motorcycle guy.

"What do you know about me?" he asked.

"I know you're an Army reject. Probably blame everyone but yourself for that."

"I'm Major Mercer. I'm First Special Forces Command. Do you know what that means, son?"

"Means that once upon a time you were a Green Beret, but then you got stuck in a hole somewhere by the MPs for committing a crime. By the looks of you, I'd guess it was for diddling boys in some foreign country. Or it was for purse-snatching. Or treason. Although now that I think about it, I bet it was for being an all-around asshole."

Widow stayed where he was. Hand still gripped on the M9. His index finger slipped into the trigger housing, glossed the skin of the trigger. He could squeeze it.

Ten rounds left. Plus one in the chamber. Ready to fire.

"Either way, I don't give a shit."

Mercer stared at Widow with no weapons in his hands, but he didn't need any. The motorcycle guy had a Glock in his hand, Harvard's Glock, Widow figured. The F150 driver had a Heckler and Koch MP5, which was an excellent gun.

Widow gripped the M9 in his hand.

Ten rounds in the magazine. One in the chamber. Two hostages and three hostiles. Two were armed and probably deadly with those weapons if any of Carr's profiles of them were true.

Major Mercer had to be armed too. He probably had a handgun under his jacket somewhere.

The odds didn't look good. There was little Widow could do without risking the Harvards' lives.

"Jack Widow, troublemaker. You sure know a lot about me. How'd you know all that? Were you sent here for us?"

Widow thought for a moment. He could lie. He could try to scare him into thinking that Widow was a part of some bigger operation.

There were Black Hawks headed their way—probably loaded up with tactical forces. Although, most likely, it was Air Force Security. The base they were flying out of was Pease Air Force Base.

A Black Hawk could travel up to two hundred something miles per hour. He knew that. He couldn't remember the exact speed, but he knew it was over two hundred miles per hour.

They were less than two hundred miles from Pease.

Carr had said thirty minutes. But getting two teams ready, locked and loaded and briefed, took time. Knowing the Air Force, it wouldn't be thirty minutes. Operations never went according to the plans of an optimistic civilian like Carr.

Carr seemed like a stand-up guy, but he was a bureaucratic pointy-head. No way did he have an actual clue how long it would take unless they had a team on standby for such an emergency.

Widow couldn't be so lucky. To his mind, it'd be more like two hours before backup reached them.

"Answer me, Widow! Stop calculating what your next move is! Your next move is whatever I tell you it is!"

"No, I wasn't sent here for you."

Widow noticed Mercer wore dog tags around his neck. Several of them.

They clanged together when he moved. Which he did right then. He pivoted on one foot and twisted, looked back at Star Harvard. He made it big and obvious for Widow to see.

Then he stepped to her, placed a heavy hand on her shoulder.

In plain sight, he made a big fist, held it up, and showed it to Widow. Then, fast, Mercer stepped over to Jackson and gut-punched him hard, like he was trying to kill him.

Mercer recoiled back just as fast as he had moved in.

Jackson heaved forward off his feet, fell to his knees, and vomited onto the concrete.

Some of it was blood.

Star screamed. For the first time since Widow had met her twenty-four hours ago, she looked like a woman broken just like that, like it was done at the snap of the fingers.

Then Mercer stepped back to her, placed his hand back on her shoulder. Same shoulder as before. She held completely still, afraid and unknowing of what to do. Her eyes stared at Widow like he had to save her. He'd save her. She knew it.

Mercer showed his fist to Widow again. That's when Widow saw he wore a knuckleduster. It was copper-colored, stained with old blood.

The three bodies at the cabin had been tortured.

The image of the knuckleduster being one tool used to interrogate the guys at the cabin flashed across his mind.

Mercer held his fist still.

He said, "I don't have time to waste on you. So I'll ask again. Are you sent here for us? Have we been compromised?"

Widow thought.

"Widow," Mercer said, "Are they waiting for us at the installation?"

Widow looked at Star's eyes.

"No!" he shouted. "No one is waiting for you."

"So, who are you? How did you know about me?"

"I'm nobody. I'm just a guy passing through."

Mercer pumped the fist like he was puffing it bigger.

He said, "Just a guy passing through?"

"That's right. I wasn't sent here by anyone. I was just here. No reason in particular."

"Like a tourist?"

"That's right. That's when I met Star Harvard. She's here looking for her husband. It seems like you found him for her."

Mercer looked at Star and then at Jackson, who was still crawling on the ground, coughing.

Mercer smiled, and then he started chuckling.

"You're just a guy. You are literally a guy in the wrong place at the wrong time."

"That's right."

"How'd you kill my guys?"

"Easy. I ambushed them."

"Where did you learn to do that?"

Widow hesitated for a moment and decided what the harm in telling him something was.

"Navy SEAL."

Mercer nodded and said, "So what? Now you're like a drifter?"

Widow nodded.

"You should join us. That's exactly why we're doing what we're doing. They use you up. Tell you it's all for patriotism, and love of country, and all that bullshit. And then they spit you out. Disgraced. Like a piece of trash."

"Major, it's time," the F150 guy said.

Mercer nodded.

"In a different life, maybe, Widow. In a different life. Maybe we could've been teammates. But not this time."

Widow stayed where he was but was ready to duck back into the house, ready for a gunfight

Ten rounds in the magazine. One in the chamber. And the sawed-off stuffed in a jacket pocket.

But the gunfight he prepared for never happened.

Mercer showed Widow the fist, again, and the knuckleduster, and said, "Drop the weapons. I won't ask twice."

Game over.

Widow exhaled and sighed and tossed the M9 out onto the grass.

"The other one too."

Widow pulled the sawed-off out and tossed it behind the M9.

"Bullets?" Mercer called out.

Widow followed the M9 and the sawed-off with the shotgun shells he had stuffed in his pockets.

Mercer lowered the fist and the knuckleduster and looked at his watch. He stared at it for several seconds.

Widow realized he was looking at a countdown.

Mercer said, "Widow, come down here."

Widow walked out and down the footpath from the front door to the driveway.

He left the front door open behind him—no reason to shut it now.

"Come close."

Widow walked close.

Mercer said, "Stand straight. Chin out."

Widow did as he asked.

In a fast, single motion, Mercer slammed his big fist into Widow's chin, knuckleduster and all. Widow flew back off his feet, tumbled to the concrete drive.

It wasn't lights out, but he was dazed and rocked like he hadn't been in recent memory.

Widow stayed on the ground for several seconds. He couldn't hear anything but ringing. It was loud, like a game show buzzer going off in his ear.

He shook his head, looked down at the concrete. It vibrated in his vision.

He steadied himself and sat back on his haunches and looked back up at Mercer, who was talking to him, but he heard nothing.

Widow reached up and felt his mouth. He checked to see if he had lost any teeth. They were all still there, probably only because Mercer hadn't hit him in the mouth.

He took deep breaths, and his hearing slowly came back, but the ringing continued. His vision still shook but slowed until everything was where it should've been, all in the right place.

"Get up."

Widow looked at Mercer.

"I said, get up!"

Widow stood back up on his feet.

"Come on."

Widow followed Mercer, who walked him over to the pickup.

"Get in."

Mercer held the driver's door open and pointed. Widow pulled himself up into the driver's seat.

"You're driving."

Widow didn't ask questions. He put his hands on the steering wheel and stayed there.

Mercer slammed the door. The F150 guy got into the back seat, directly behind Widow. He pointed the MP5 at the back of the seat.

Jackson Harvard was forced into the passenger side, front, next to Widow.

Mercer got up close to the window and said, "You're going to drive us in."

Mercer looked at his watch and then showed it to Widow.

There was a digital countdown on it in big, blue numbers. It read fifteen minutes left.

"We got to be at the entrance hatch in fifteen minutes, which means no time for sightseeing. You don't stop. You ram right through the front gates."

"The guards will shoot us down if we floor it into the gate."

"Why do you think you're driving first?"

Mercer hopped off the truck and slapped the hood twice with his hand.

Widow put the seatbelt on.

The guy behind him shoved the MP5 forward and up and into the back of Widow's head.

"You don't need that. Neither of you."

Widow looked at Jackson. They had both been buckling up. They both let go of their seatbelts.

Widow looked into the rearview.

"What do we call you?"

"My name's Arnold. Not that it matters."

Widow asked, "Was Lareno your pal?"

Arnold said nothing.

Widow said, "He died like a coward. So that you know."

"Stop talking. Start the engine. Let's go. Down that road."

Widow nodded and started the engine. He looked up and watched the motorcycle guy get on the bike, start it up, and drive off to the road. Then Mercer grabbed Star by the arm. He shoved her into the driver's seat of the Jeep. He hopped in on the passenger side.

Mercer and Star backed the Jeep up and pulled alongside Widow.

Mercer smiled and said, "You first."

Widow stayed quiet. He put the F150 in drive and peeled away from the curb, headed down the road to the installation.

34

THEY SPED DOWN THE ROAD, kicking up gravel and dust clouds. Trees lined the sides.

Widow was at the front of the caravan of vehicles. Besides the F150, the motorcycle, and Star and Mercer in the Jeep, they were joined by another F150 that had been parked across the road like a roadblock.

Halfway to the installation, they passed another pickup, parked off the road. Widow saw two men standing in the bed and lined up on top of the truck. Resting on a rifle bipod was a Barrett fifty-caliber sniper rifle, a vicious weapon.

This one had a massive scope on it. It was boxy and electronic.

Widow guessed they used it to spy on the installation, probably night work to keep from being spotted.

They drove on.

Widow looked over at Jackson.

"You're Jackson?"

"Yeah."

"For the last twenty-four hours, we thought you were dead."

Jackson stared over at him.

"I'm sorry. I hid out. They ambushed my crew two nights ago at our house. We share a house. I came home late, saw what was happening, and ran."

Widow didn't make any judgments.

"I'm so sorry," Jackson said, again like he was apologizing to his dead crew.

"Don't apologize to me."

Silence.

Then Jackson asked, "You've been helping my wife?"

"Yeah. I just met her yesterday. She was alone. I thought the gentlemanly thing to do was help."

"Thank you for that."

Widow looked in the rearview mirror at Arnold. The guy listened to them intently. He was staring back at Widow in the mirror.

Widow asked, "Out of curiosity, where were you hiding?"

"Motel row. I figured I could blend in with the lumberjacks."

"Why didn't you call anyone?"

"We're not supposed even to be here. I didn't know who to call."

Widow didn't know what to say to that. It sounded weak to him. It sounded more like Jackson was too scared to call anyone. Too frightened to help his friends. After all, he stopped calling his eight-months-pregnant wife over a month ago, long before some terrorists captured his crew.

Jackson struck him as a man who maybe used to be strong, but now he was cowardly.

Widow almost spoke up about it, but what was the point? Here they were. They were in this together now.

"Stop talking," Arnold barked.

A moment of silence passed, and then Arnold said, "Here we go. Get ready."

Widow looked forward. They came over a hill, kicking up a ton more dust clouds.

Up ahead, Widow had a clear view of the installation. It wasn't much to look at. There were two buildings, both tan, both brick, both very plain. From the air, they probably looked like dull, forgotten utility sheds.

A single radio antenna shot up into the air.

A tall chain-link fence surrounded the installation. Barbed razor wire coiled at the top prevented climbers.

Widow saw the gate. It was a simple chain-link gate that opened inward.

Two MPs stood out front. Both were armed with M4 carbines. They were laced up tight with body armor and helmets. Only two visible guards, but they were serious looking.

Widow said, "They'll shoot us dead."

Arnold said, "Don't you worry. Just speed up. Ram them."

Widow wouldn't run down two men in uniform.

He had to do something. But what?

"Speed up!" Arnold barked.

Widow sped up, but slowly. He kept his foot as far off the pressure as he could, trying to buy time. What was he going to do?

He was only buying seconds, but every second counted.

He could think of nothing. There was no way out.

They were closing in now. A hundred yards. Eighty yards. Seventy yards. The speedometer kicked up speed. The dial was rising slowly.

Widow peeked in the rearview mirror. He saw the dust clouds kicking up thick and stormy.

That's when he thought of the sniper rifle. They were going to shoot the guards from long range.

But the dust clouds. Maybe he could save them. He could create a huge smokescreen.

Widow punched it. He stomped his foot down as hard as he could. He loosened his grip on the wheel, trying to let the truck fishtail wildly, riotously, madly. And it did.

The bed swerved from side to side like a dog wagging a tail.

Massive clouds of dust kicked up into the air. The dust rose so thick that Widow could see Star slowing in the rearview to avoid driving blind.

The motorcycle guy did the same until they were all swallowed up by the dust.

In a fast, almost violent movement, Widow reached up and grabbed the seatbelt with one hand and buckled it.

Fifty yards. Forty. Thirty. Twenty. Ten.

"Jackson! Get down!"

Jackson hunched over and ducked down against the center console.

Widow grabbed Jackson's head and pushed him down, bracing him for impact.

The MPs started firing their M4s—all full auto.

A spray of bullets tore through the F150's hood and ate into the engine block.

Widow ducked down, covering Jackson.

At the last five yards, he swerved the wheel.

Bullets sprayed into the cabin, into the dashboard, and into the rear bench.

The truck didn't flip like Widow had planned, but it swerved right and slammed through a barricade and the chain-link gate, and crashed, hard, into one building, rocking it to the core.

No way did the airman on-post not feel it.

Which was what he hoped for. He hoped they'd all come running out, locked and loaded. But he couldn't have been more wrong.

35

Widow heard yelling and shouting. The guards were barking commands at the F150, demanding he come out with his hands up.

He was still on his side, covering Jackson, who was breathing. He was alive.

Widow slowly got up. The windshield was cracked and spiderwebbed beyond recognition. He could barely see out of it in most places. What he could see was that the truck's fender was smashed to bits. There were pieces of brick falling off the sidewall of the building he'd rammed.

The truck's hood was riddled with bullet holes.

Smoke steamed out of them. He smelled leaking oil, mixed with water, mixed with engine fluids.

The tires were blown, all of them.

It was a good thing that he'd fallen over Jackson because the steering wheel was crushed inward about six inches. He checked Jackson, who seemed all in one piece, but was unconscious, or at least not moving.

The guards continued to bark orders.

More were piling out of the buildings. They weren't all guards, but they were all armed with something. Some had assault rifles; some had handguns; some even had kitchen utensils.

Widow raised his hands so that they could be seen. He jerked his legs out from under the steering wheel. The footwell was safe, but the wheel got him a little stuck. After he got his feet up and out, he reached down and clicked the door handle, kicked the door open.

More screaming and yelling at him to come out slowly.

Widow hauled himself out of the truck.

It took him a second to get oriented. Then he did.

First, he looked at Arnold in the backseat. He was dead.

Widow knew that because the guy's neck was snapped and his head was over to one side, the wrong side. It looked like the seatbelt had somehow ridden up to his neck. Or he slumped down too far. The belt had locked up like it was supposed to do, but the side impact into the brick wall had jolted it. He sailed into it like he was hitting a clothesline at a hundred miles per hour, which technically was pretty close to the truth of the situation.

The MPs were still yelling at Widow. That ringing in his ears was back and angrier, as if it had just rested and now was woken back up.

Widow stood up, hands in the air, but then he froze and turned so fast that the MPs almost shot him from the sudden movement.

He looked at the dust clouds. They loomed enormously over the road and the broken gate.

The smokescreen had worked, or so he thought.

But just then, he heard the loud, deafening sound of a sniper rifle. The Barrett was unmistakable.

The sound broke all others. It overrode the ringing in his ears.

Widow heard several shots. He couldn't keep track.

Boom! Boom! Boom!

They kept going. A second apart. Either the sniper they had was super-fast, or the Barrett didn't have bolt-action, which it may not have. He couldn't recall.

Widow turned back to the guards.

He watched in utter horror as one by one; they were ripped off their feet.

He watched one's head get torn clean off.

The next one's chest burst open.

Another's torso from his solar plexus to his right arm and shoulder was torn clean off.

The bodies flew back several feet.

The box on the Barrett's scope must have thermals.

The smokescreen did nothing to stop the sniper.

All it did was create enough confusion to slow down Warren and Mercer and Star.

Widow slunk down, lowering his profile. If the sniper was using thermals, he'd not know who was who.

Widow's first instinct was to grab an M4. It lay on the ground by the dismembered arm of one of the MPs. But he decided not to. Not yet.

That was probably how the sniper was deciphering his targets. None of the guys he was supposed to shoot were carrying rifles.

Widow went back to the truck, looked over the seat, and took the MP5, a submachine gun with a smaller profile. The sniper might think he was Arnold.

He checked the weapon. It was fully loaded.

Then he snuck around to the passenger door. He had to scramble over the hood of the truck, kicking brick out of the way.

The Barrett continued to fire, taking out every airman who ran out of the Air Force buildings.

Widow had not counted the dead bodies or the gunshots. But five seconds later, he was standing above Jackson, trying to wake him, when he realized that the Barrett had stopped firing.

He figured they might've killed everyone in the compound except for the missileers fifty feet below in the silo, who were under thick concrete and steel. They probably didn't know what was happening on the surface.

Jackson was out cold. He wasn't faking it. Widow grabbed him under the arms and jerked him, yanked him out of the truck, and dragged him away from the rubble.

He dragged him fifty-plus feet and hauled him far to the back of the building.

There was a metal door. Widow opened it and checked it. No one was there. It opened to a back hallway.

Widow dragged Jackson inside and into a room. It was an office. There was a sofa. He rolled Jackson onto it and left him.

He ran down the hall, calling out.

"Is anyone here?"

No answer.

"Anyone here?"

No answer.

Widow ran from one end to the other, looking for survivors. There was no one. The building was empty.

He headed for the front door, but it was unpassable because one end of the truck had crushed the wall over it.

Widow ran back the other way and out the back door.

He huddled close to the back wall and looked at the gate. The dust was settling, wafting, and subsiding.

He saw the Jeep come through the gate, then the motorcycle guy. They parked their vehicles, and Mercer jerked Star out of the Jeep. He held her by the arm.

The motorcycle man waited at the busted gate. One minute later, three other men came driving through it in another pickup truck.

The Barrett was in the hand of one guy. He was the sniper. The magazine was gone from the rifle.

The driver of the truck K-turned and pointed the nose out the gate onto the road.

The sniper reloaded the Barrett and took the same firing position that he had before, only now he was covering the road, a precaution to fight off cops or whoever might come.

The good news was the cavalry coming, the guys loaded into two Black Hawks. They weren't driving up a road.

The bad news was a Barrett fifty-caliber can fire through an engine block of an Army transport truck, which meant that he could blow the Black Hawks out of the sky from long range.

The worse news was that none of that mattered because the cavalry wouldn't make it in time. Mercer's countdown had said fifteen minutes, which was about fifteen minutes ago.

The missileers were coming up any minute, thinking that they were ending a forty-eight-hour shift.

Widow had to get to them first. There must be a security check where they radioed up before coming up.

He took the MP5 and ran back around the building, staying out of sight.

He hid behind trees and rocks and gullies and anything else he could find.

Then in the back of the other building, he saw the entrance to the shaft that led down to the missileers. It was a platform that came up out of the ground. It was all concrete.

It looked like a concrete pit that led down to an elevator.

Where was the communications room?

Then he heard voices from behind.

He saw Mercer, and three of the four guys he'd brought and Star. He held her from behind. There was a gun in his hand. It was weird. It looked like a short-barreled shotgun, but it was different.

Widow focused on it.

It was a modified nail gun.

The situation was bad, but Widow had dealt with bad before.

Just then, it got much worse.

The elevator doors made a noise, and a few seconds later, they opened.

Mercer stared at his watch. A big smile came over his face.

The motorcycle guy held a big radio in his hand. He must've done the security check with the missileers before they came up. Somehow, they had already hacked into the process.

Widow didn't know how, but the details didn't matter. He was out of time. Mercer was going to fire at least five nuclear-tipped Minuteman III ICBMs. He was going to fire US nuclear missiles, and probably at US targets.

The two missileers stood in sheer terror when they saw the carnage above.

36

MERCER POINTED the nail gun at the missileers.

"We're going back down, fellas," he said.

Widow watched him, and another guy, the one who was with the sniper, walk over to the missileers, who were trembling and protesting.

Widow couldn't hear them.

He couldn't let Mercer get down that shaft. If he made it into the silo, Widow had no idea how to stop him. He seriously doubted that he could break into a nuclear missile-firing silo, deemed so top-secret that ninety-nine point nine percent of the top brass didn't even know it existed.

No way.

He had to act fast. He had to act now. Or it was all over.

Widow stood up and ran back around the undamaged building. He stayed close to the wall. He ran at full-sprint speed.

He switched the fire selector on the MP5 to full auto.

By the time he came around the corner, back to the destroyed gate, he was panting hard.

Widow didn't stop for breath. He ran and ran.

He came right up behind the pickup with the sniper.

The sniper was facing the empty road ahead. He was staring over the Barrett's scope, waiting for whoever was about to come so he could take them out.

He heard sprinting steps behind him, but he assumed it was one of his teammates.

It wasn't.

Widow scrambled up the back of the truck.

The sniper spun around and saw him. He dropped his grip on the rifle and snatched a Glock out of a hip holster.

Widow was faster.

Widow fired the MP5 into the sniper's chest. He pressed the trigger down and fired five rounds in quick succession.

Pop! Pop! They went.

Prescott's chest burst open into five separate bullet holes, spraying red mist back at Widow.

No time.

Widow dropped the MP5 and ripped the Barrett off the roof of the truck. He left the bipod down.

Widow ran back, leaped off the truck's bed, over the tailgate. He hit the dirt hard, but landed on his feet. He kept running, past the dead MPs, through the buildings, past the wrecked F150, and the dead Arnold.

Mercer, Warrens, Allen, Jones, Star, and the two missileers all turned and stared at the cloud of dust pluming up from someone running at them like a ghost in smoke.

Widow stopped dead, fell to one knee.

Time slowed down.

He ignored everyone but Mercer.

He ignored the rifle's scope. He didn't need it, and it'd be tuned incorrectly for this close range. He aimed over the rifling and the barrel to the side of the scope.

It turned out the Barrett wasn't bolt-action after all because he fired in a fast chain of destruction like a madman, only he was a madman who could shoot straight and damn good.

He fired the first round at Mercer.

The *boom*! from the first round probably saved his life because it stunned everyone but him.

The bullet ripped through the center of Mercer's face, decapitating half his head. It created a massive crater where the man's nose used to be. Forget about the H-shaped scars on his face. They were gone, along with most of his facial features.

The dog tags came flying off his neck, and the rest of the body crumpled back and fell onto the floor of the elevator.

Widow didn't pause there.

He moved left, fired another round, and killed the one called Allen.

Then Widow jerked right, fired another round at the one called Jones.

Both men flew back off their feet. The bullets tore holes in both men the size of a paper cup's rim from the front and exited through their backs, leaving holes the size of barstools.

Red mist splattered and sprayed everywhere.

The last man standing from Mercer's group was the motorcycle guy, Warrens. He reacted, jerked up Star's Glock, and aimed it at Widow. He fired in panic, and the first round went past Widow and slammed into the brick wall of one building.

Before Widow could fire another round at Warrens, Star kicked the guy in the back of the knees. He toppled down onto his knees. She lunged on top of him.

Behind Warrens, while Widow was killing the others, she had scooped up a pile of dirt. Now she shoved it into his face, over his sunglasses and behind them.

He started punching the air. She dodged his blows and scooped up her Glock.

She fired three rounds into his gut and one in his chest.

Warrens stopped moving. He was dead.

Star Harvard holstered the Glock, turned to Widow, and ran over to him. The pregnancy didn't stop her. He stood up, dropped the Barrett, and intercepted her.

She slammed into him, hugged him close.

Widow looked over her shoulder. He looked over the dead terrorists and then up at the two missileers.

They stood there, still holding their hands up. They stared down at the beheaded Mercer, and they looked at each other, completely dumbfounded.

37

Widow hugged Star Harvard tight. They found Jackson coming to inside. He shook hands with Widow, telling him he couldn't express how grateful he was.

Widow told them he didn't want to wait around. He didn't want to be part of debriefings and reports and interviews and bureaucrats.

Star hugged him twice before he left.

She asked where he would go. He shrugged and left on Warrens' motorcycle.

Why not? he thought.

Riding back to town, Widow saw Deputy Cole passing him by, headed back the way he'd come. Probably to Dorothy's house.

He felt bad for her. She had it as bad as anyone from all this.

He pressed on. The wind blew through his short hair.

When Widow got to the edge of Hellbent, he passed the road with the unmarked grave.

He should've kept riding, but he felt he needed to know.

So he turned and headed to the barbershop.

Widow parked the bike on the curb and went in.

The barber was there.

He looked at Widow, who was a bloody mess.

"Well, you look like you've been in a war."

"I have. Basically."

"Did you find that airman?"

"I did. He's alive."

"I'm guessing that you won?"

"I did."

"Bad guys?"

"They walk among the angels now. Or not."

The barber nodded.

Widow said, "So what's the deal with the grave?"

"It's an old grave. From two hundred years ago, or so the legend goes."

"So, what's the big deal?"

"She was a teenage mother who was burned at the stake. Accused of witchcraft."

Widow listened.

The barber said, "This is a deeply religious town. At least the older people are, and they're the ones in charge."

"So?"

"So the young witch wasn't just burned at the stake. The family was cursed with shame. And the witch's grave was set up as a constant reminder of that shame. And even today, no one is allowed to alter the grave."

Widow said, "That's nuts."

The barber shrugged, said, "It stays where it is. It is as it is."

Widow looked at the floor and then up at the barber.

He asked, "The name of the woman?"

"Mable."

"As in Mable's Diner?"

The barber nodded.

That's why the lumberjacks and Mable were so bent out of shape when he asked about it. It was a sore subject for her.

Widow thanked the barber and left.

He mounted the motorcycle, checked the gas tank gauge, and rode away.

* * *

ONE HOUR LATER, two Air Force Black Hawks flew into Hellbent. They were fully loaded with MPs armed to the teeth. They arrived at a secret installation that nobody was supposed to know about. They found six dead terrorists and a half dozen dead MPs and servicemen and three living missileers, one who was barefoot and conscious. He was holding on to his wife, of whom was more than eight months pregnant. She looked like she was ready to give birth at any moment.

BLACK DAYLIGHT: A PREVIEW

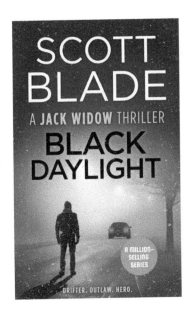

Out Now!

BLACK DAYLIGHT: A BLURB

A heinous crime.

One witness—Jack Widow.

One suspect—Jack Widow.

A snowy night. A lonely country road. The Black Hills of South Dakota. Widow takes a wrong turn and witnesses the aftermath of a heinous crime. The only trace he sees of the criminals is a pair of taillights.

A simple crime turns Widow into a local sheriff's one and only suspect, but nothing is as it seems.

Trying to prove his innocence, Widow's need to right wrongs dredges up a hidden network of pure evil.

Fans of Lee Child's **Jack Reacher**, Vince Flynn's **Mitch Rapp**, and Mark Greaney's **The Gray Man** will love this installment of the million-selling Jack Widow thriller series.

Readers are saying...

★★★★★ Black Daylight is engrossing and difficult to put down! It's a good thing I'm on vacation!

★★★★★ Widow is one guy you don't mess with!

CHAPTER 1

KILLING A LOVED one in cold blood was harder than they thought. It wasn't like shooting a pedestrian in the street or killing a stranger, or a nobody, stealing his wallet and driving off, unnoticed, unidentified, anonymous, unscathed.

It isn't like murder, even though it is murder. Killing a loved one squeezes a little more out of the words *cold-blooded* than other kinds of murder.

They knew that because they had felt it.

Killing her shouldn't have been like killing a dog either. But that's how they went about it.

They put her down in the same way that a vet kills an animal, carelessly, compassionless, sterile. They murdered her with no regard for her relation to them, without empathy, without remorse.

It was still hard, though.

At first, it had been different. At first, they had two problems with killing the girl.

One, the act itself, the "killing" part, not the concept, but the "how to do it" part of the whole thing. And second, the "getting away with it" part, which was the most important part.

What was the point of premeditated murder if they couldn't get away with it?

Premeditated murder without the "getting away with it" part was like calling their drug dealer and not knowing what they wanted to order, a problem that they never had.

Their problem had always been paying for the drugs, not deciding what to get.

In the end, they strangled the girl and dumped out the body in what they considered being the middle of nowhere, which was also everything around them. They lived in the middle of nowhere. Compared to other states, theirs was mostly ignored, except for one busy attraction, Mount Rushmore, but not this time of year—too cold.

Strangled and dumped like a dog. That's how it would be seen on a police report if it ever got seen on a police report. That's how it would be reported in a newspaper if it ever saw a newspaper. But that's not exactly how it went down.

What a police report or the newspapers wouldn't say is how hard it was to do, how much strength it took.

Loved one or not. Killing someone is hard enough for most people, especially their first time, and this had been their first time.

Strangling a loved one to death happens in only two ways.

The first is a crime of passion. It's done in the heat of the moment, like an explosion of emotion and rage and indignation and hate and love, all at once, all straight from the gut, like a volcano erupting or an earthquake rattling the ground below. There's little warning if any, but the results are the same—deadly and messy and unstoppable.

Killing a loved one comes from a place of love. They knew that. One of them did, anyway. That was a big part of their rationalization for the whole thing, but it wasn't rationalization. It was twisted backward logic.

They loved her.

They were doing this for her, in a way. That was the twisted logic, they told themselves. And they believed it.

They brainwashed themselves into rationalizing it this way, like a man on death row, confessing his sins to the chaplain, thinking it would make a difference, hoping it would make a difference, but knowing in his gut that the end was the same.

Convincing themselves to follow through with it was as much an act of desperation as the killing itself.

There was another thing, another question they asked themselves over and over. It was the question that started the whole thing.

What was the girl going to do with all that money, anyway?

She had a large sum of money coming to her. But why? Why should she get it and not them? What had she ever done to deserve it?

That amount of money was enough to set them up for a lifetime. At least, that's what they thought.

The money was better off with them, and she was better off dead. She had nothing to live for, after all. No husband. No kids. No prospects for a husband.

All she had in her life was them and a little dog, and some plans to get out of there, to move on to some place, maybe college, she had mentioned.

That was a joke.

What college would take her? She was a reformed meth-head from South Dakota. And she was barely reformed. She was more like one foot out of the grave.

No, that money was better off with them.

The money was the ultimate reason, the motive for killing her. Without it, they would've never come up with the whole scheme.

Still, they told themselves it wasn't just about the money. They told themselves it was out of love.

How could they kill a loved one without love?

That was what they asked themselves.

The whole business was like how people talk themselves into committing suicide. It calls for backward and sideways logic.

Initially, a person jokes about suicide, maybe months before, maybe years before he or she actually goes through with it. Maybe it comes up on impulse, at first. Maybe they're stoned or drunk during the inception of suicidal thoughts.

Unlike most thoughts, this one doesn't leave them.

It lingers within them like a weed in the grass.

After mulling it over, eventually, the weed grows and grows until they've brainwashed themselves into thinking that suicide is a good idea until they convince themselves it's the only choice they have left.

It's the only way out.

With someone contemplating suicide, there comes a line that once crossed; there's no turning back.

Suicide is premeditated murder. It gets planned and thought of and rationalized, until that plan, that thought, that rationalization, becomes reality, and then someone dies.

The loved ones also twisted that old saying: *There's a thin line between love and hate*, to help rationalize it.

A thin line between love and hate.

That's where her murder took place. Somewhere between love and hate. Somewhere on that thin line.

The loved ones didn't go about killing her in that first crime-of-passion way.

They didn't get the urge to kill in a fit of rage. It was no accident. No one lost control and did the deed that way.

They planned it.

They fed themselves the delusion that it was out of love for weeks leading up to the act, but they killed her for money—plain and simple.

What other reason did they need?

They planned the whole thing out, as best as two people like them could plan it out.

When it was finally time, it made total sense to them. The way the plan was laid out, they could get away with it.

Why not?

Who was going to catch them?

People got away with murder all the time. Every day. They saw the news. They saw the true crime shows on TV. They had social media, saw the retweeted and reposted news stories.

Plus, they had grown up here, a big state with lots of rural, rugged, mountainous areas and pockets of thick forest. They heard the stories. People died all the time where they lived.

Part of the beauty of their plan was that no one else knew about the money.

It wasn't insurance money. She had no life insurance—no pending lawsuit that would award a large payout upon a final court decision.

There was no inheritance coming her way.

If she had ever been found, there was nothing to tie the murder to them. They had no visible motive. There was nothing to gain by killing her. Nothing that anyone could see. No cops. Certainly not the county sheriff's department. They had that part locked down.

There was nothing on paper.

The money was untraceable because it wasn't coming from a legal source. Therefore, no one could track it. No one could find it. No one even knew about it, except the three of them, and one of them was about to die.

That was the beauty of it all. It was all secret: untraceable, secret money, a payment that only she was expecting for her efforts, a payment that they planned to kill her for.

Kill her and take the money. Easy-peasy.

Even though they planned it out, they had to be smart about it—no question. They had watched cop shows. They had watched the forensic shows. They knew that to get away with murder, you must get rid of the body. That part was crucial. It was imperative. The whole plan depended on it.

No body. No evidence. No crime.

That was the second mistake they made.

The first mistake they made was they thought they could kill her sober, without drugs. They thought that staying sober was key in order to make sure every little detail was accounted for, and all loose ends were tied off—the right way.

Once they did one hit, or one bump, or shot up, or popped a pill, eventually they'd lose their sobriety, lose their senses, and they couldn't let that happen. That's how mistakes get made. Everything would be reduced, and for murder, they figured it best to keep all brain functions working optimally.

But that was mistake number one.

They stayed sober all day long, waiting for when the completion of the money transaction came, waiting for the funds to be in hand, waiting for the moment to strike.

It started that morning for her, but for them, it had started the day before because they couldn't sleep the whole night long. They had too much anxiety; too much rode on getting everything just right.

The whole procedure was delicate after all, not the murder, but the part before, the part that the buyers needed before they would even hand over the money.

The buyers were an X-factor that they didn't expect, and they worried about it. Only the girl had spoken with them. They knew from the conversations with the girl that the buyers were serious, dangerous people. They were not the kind of people to be trifled with. When they first met the buyers, that assumption was proven correct.

The buyers turned out to be two guys. They claimed to represent the actual buyer, who they knew nothing about, and neither did the girl.

The buyers never revealed their names, at least not their real names. That's how it came off because the names they gave were generic—John Smith and Joe Smith.

The fake names might've been more believable if the men had been white or American, but they were neither. That was clear.

Neither of the men was American, not in the born and raised sense of things.

The two men were both dark-skinned and appeared Arabic, and they had accents, but not the Middle Eastern Arabic kind that they had seen in movies or on TV. These guys had accents closer to British than anything else, but they weren't from India. That was obvious.

They were from somewhere in the Middle East, maybe Saudi Arabia, one of the loved ones figured, with no real evidence or reasoning behind it. It just sounded right to them.

The buyers wore clean, pressed suits and ties. The suits were expensive, tailored pieces. They were customized to give enormous leeway so they could provide the wearer with room to move and fight.

The suits were tactical, like something James Bond might wear.

One suit was brown and the other straight black. Both ties were black. Both were clip-ons because the United States Secret Service agents only wore clip-ons. In close-quarters combat, the clip-on tie keeps the wearer from being choked with his own tie.

The buyers came off like soldiers because their behavior seemed bellicose and militaristic.

The buyers were armed. They had shoulder rigs under their coats, presumably with special-forces-grade firearms holstered in them.

After they met, the buyers, the loved ones, and the girl all waited in a ventilated, abandoned tire garage on the side of a road that was nothing more than a lonely turnoff from another lonely road that spider-webbed somewhere between the town of Deadwood and a sleepy town called Reznor.

They were closer to Deadwood than Reznor.

The buyers and the girl had scheduled the whole procedure to take place at this location. It was an agreed spot. It was abandoned, concealed from the main roads, and well ventilated. Plus, it had ample space for all the medical equipment that would be needed for a successful transaction.

The buyers were good at their jobs. Their entire organization was good at what they did. So, they did more of the suggesting of the location than the girl did, but they let her think she had input.

Unbeknownst to the girl and her killers, the buyers had scouted the location out beforehand.

Of course they had. They were professionals. They oversaw this kind of transaction all the time. At least once a week, they were on the road, somewhere in America, or Canada, and sometimes even Mexico, doing what they do.

Sometimes they oversaw transactions, and sometimes they dealt with problems—all part of the job description.

The buyers had mapped it, scouted it, and even timed the ambulance response. They'd arrived a day earlier and called nine-one-one to a similar distance from Deadwood and waited. When the paramedics arrived, they clocked the arrival time as seventeen minutes, give or take ten seconds. It was a good arrival time, considering that they were so far out from Deadwood.

Beyond Deadwood's city limits was nothing but empty roads, thick forests, and quiet people who liked to be left alone.

Once outside the city, the ambulance could pick up speed. They could probably drive close to triple digits on the speedometer gauge for several minutes before reaching a curve in the road or seeing another car.

After the procedure was over, the buyers were reluctant to hand over the money at first. They sensed that the loved ones weren't the most trustworthy people to chaperone the girl, who would need immediate medical attention.

Something didn't feel right to them, but she had come with them. She had picked them to be her guardians after the procedure was over. She had vouched for them. And she had lived up to her part of the deal. In this business, a deal was a deal. They got what they came for. Now it was time to pay up.

The buyers paid, and left instructions to call nine-one-one ten minutes after they left.

They packed up all their equipment. Watched as the medical crew drove away, waited five more minutes till the coast was clear, and they were left alone with the girl, still unconscious from the sedatives, and her chaperones.

The doctor had left a bottle of painkillers for the girl. The loved ones were going to keep that for themselves, naturally.

The buyers and the chaperones shook hands. Deal done, and the buyers handed over the money. They didn't wait for it to be counted; they drove off in a Chevy Impala, with the product they came for in hand, safely stored away in the proper container.

The buyers told the chaperones to wait ten more minutes and then call the emergency services. They explained the ambulance would come and they would take her to the hospital.

The buyers explained no one would get in trouble. The chaperones had broken no laws. It was the buyers who would get into trouble if caught. They were the ones breaking laws.

The buyers also made it clear what would happen to the chaperones if they snitched if the buyers were caught. They made a threat in a "keep quiet or else" kind of conversation.

The buyers weren't joking around either. They made that clear, too—no need to show off their sidearms. The whole spectacle—the shoulder rigs, the firearms, the expensive car, the tailored suits, the medical crew, and a large amount of untraceable cash—said it all.

The chaperones knew that. They could see it. It was obvious even to a couple of rural meth-heads like them.

After the coast was clear, the buyers were long gone, and before they killed her, they had to decide on how to do it. But first, they did what any junkie would do; they reveled in the money.

It came in a medium-sized black duffle bag. They opened it, stared at it, stayed quiet, and stared some more. They couldn't bring themselves to count it, but they touched it. They moved it around and studied the stacks of cash. It was all big bills, easy enough to transport and easy enough to spend.

After the reality of being a step away kicked in, they turned back to what they had to do. The money wasn't quite theirs yet. They had to kill the girl.

They were still on the fence about how to go about it.

There were many ways to do it.

The best way would've been to just open her up from her stitches right there, and let her bleed out. No one would've pinned it on them.

But they couldn't do it that way. The trail might lead the cops to the buyers, and the buyers had already told them what that would mean for them.

Before they strangled her, they got nervous again. They got cold feet. They got the jitters—brought on by the act of killing someone and because they had both been sober for twenty-four hours, and that was twice longer than they were used to.

Like any junkie, they didn't make it to their goal of staying sober until after the deed was done. So they blazed up right there.

The meth they had wasn't particularly good. It was low quality, bottom-of-the-barrel type stuff, but it did the trick. They could buy better-quality meth later. With the money they just got paid, they could keep themselves in the good stuff for years.

The decision to strangle her came because they convinced themselves it was the hardest to track back to them.

First instinct was to shoot her. They had come armed. One of them had a gun. He always had a gun, but the deliberations changed their minds. They decided. No guns. No bullets. No knives. They talked themselves out of using weapons completely.

Weapons have handles and retain fingerprints and hair follicles and dirt and grime—too much forensic evidence.

They didn't want to get caught. Obviously.

What good was a bunch of money if you get caught?

Can't spend it in prison. Although, one of them commented they could get meth in prison, probably. They started a short argument over the idea, which caused them to blaze up one more time. It was more of the bad meth. This led to more deliberations, until they came back full circle to the original method of murder that they had already vaguely planned on.

They had to strangle her. That was the right way to do it.

And it would be easy enough. She couldn't fight back. She was too doped up.

Truth be told, they all were at this point. But she was seriously doped up even though they had done meth twice.

The stuff she was on took the cake. It was all medical-grade, high-quality stuff.

The buyer's medical crew sedated her with serious medications.

They remembered hearing words like Prednisone and Fentanyl and Alfentanil and Meperidine. None of which they understood, but then they heard words like Oxycodone and Diamorphine, and they knew those.

They didn't know which was used.

They didn't know what any of them were. They weren't doctors. They weren't college-educated. They weren't even high school educated. Not really. Both of them had dropped out.

All they knew was that the meds she had in her bloodstream knocked her out cold, and she wasn't getting back up soon.

She wouldn't fight back.

After they decided on the method of death, they discussed disposal.

They could kill her and dump her on the side of the road.

One of them suggested that right off, but the other one rejected the idea. It was too easy for her to be found that way. There had to be more to it.

Some effort was needed.

The other one suggested they should do more to conceal the body, like bury it or stuff her with rocks and send her over the edge of a boat into a lake. Maybe they could incinerate her in a giant oven or a kiln like the ones used in morgues.

"Whatever that oven's called," one of them had said.

After a while, after all the deliberating, after it became apparent to both of them they were stalling, they came to an agreement.

It was time.

First thing was first. They had to kill her.

As their highs wore off, which was due more to the severity of the situation than the quality or quantity of the meth in their systems, they almost couldn't do it.

The physically stronger of the two of them hesitated. Then he chickened out. The smaller one couldn't do it either.

In the end, they opened the duffle bag to stare at the money again, like a motivator. They could still turn back. The girl would never know.

The smaller one opened the duffle bag. They both stared again at the stacks of hundred-dollar bills, bound tight with currency bands. It was all unmarked, and all theirs if they wanted it, if they did what had to be done.

Finally, the smaller one pushed harder at the stronger one.

"Okay. Now. It's time," the smaller one said.

The stronger one nodded, and he did the killing.

First, he opened the painkillers intended for the girl and popped a couple. He stuffed the rest in his coat pocket, safe for later.

He walked over to the girl, pulled her off a cheap hospital bed the crew provided for her. She hit her head on the way down on the corner of the table. That had been an accident. Blood seeped out of a large cut. At first, they thought she might die from that. They hoped, but she didn't.

It wasn't deep enough. It was superficial, at worst.

The stronger one ignored the cut. No reason to patch her up, and he climbed on top of her, straddled her for a long moment. He held his hands up above her face. They shook and trembled violently for a long moment. His nerves rattled like jittering stones. He felt a pounding in his head that came on slowly, but far away at first, like a distant runner on pavement.

He closed his eyes tight and reached his hands out, gripped them around her throat, and strangled her.

She didn't resist. She never woke up. He strangled her until he thought she was dead.

Once her body seemed to go lifeless, deliberations were pointless. Deciding to dump the body was easy. It didn't matter.

They had a good idea of where to take her, and it wasn't a lake or a grave.

The Ninety has a three-hundred-and-forty-mile stretch of road that passes through the state. This stretch of road was notorious for harboring dead bodies.

They had watched a special on it one night, back when they were only joking about the idea of murder.

The special aired on KOTA, the ABC affiliate out of Rapid City, but that's not where they saw it. They had originally watched it on the internet. It popped up when they were searching Google, trying to get ideas about where to dump the body. It appeared right there in front of them, like an answer to a prayer.

Four months ago, the KOTA news team did a piece on I-Ninety called "Death Road."

They watched the whole thing, one of the few times that either of them had ever watched a complete news story while sober.

The special shocked them. It was an amazing piece. Incredibly, over the last thirty years, more than two hundred dead bodies had been discovered there.

Although it turned out that for some of them, there had been logical explanations: hikers frozen to death, or hikers eaten by bears, or hikers eaten by wolves, and so on.

Not all of them were so easily explained. Many of them had been murdered and dumped and stripped of clothes, which the loved ones figured was to get rid of trace evidence.

Some murders seemed to be connected, some by the nudity of the bodies. Some were found rolled up in rugs, some stuffed in trunks, and others wrapped up in plastic.

The news team tried to play it up like they had uncovered the dumping ground of an unknown serial killer, a mysterious killer out there somewhere. He was prowling hitchhikers, runaways, and nobodies. He raped the women, killed them, and dumped the bodies.

That was how the media had reported it, sensationalized it.

None of it was true, though. Many of the dead had been drug-related murders or thefts gone wrong or many other scenarios, and they weren't all women, either. They had found plenty of dead men. None of it was the work of a mysterious serial killer.

The truth didn't stop their imaginations from running wild over the story.

It led them to wild ideas. It led them to many possibilities about how to go about the girl's disposal.

That same night they watched the online news video, they smoked some heavy crystal, better than what they had now, and they sat back and talked about it.

One of them said, "You know if you wanted to hide a body, just do it off the Ninety."

The next one said, "You can even go farther and drive off one of the country roads. There are hundreds of dead ends out there. Lots of unknown dirt roads."

"Empty roads with nothing on them."

The smaller one took a deep puff from the meth, inhaled, and smiled.

"Nobody would ever find the body."

"Who would you kill?"

When the answer came, it shocked the stronger one. He played it off as a joke. And it was a joke, at first, but then they started talking about money.

How could they make a bunch of money? If there was money to be made, then it might not be a joke.

This conversation went on like this for weeks and weeks until the answer fell in their lap like it had been dropped there by the gods themselves.

The idea came from the most unlikely place.

The soon-to-be victim gave them the idea.

It turned out that she had also been thinking of ways to make fast money. The route that she had contemplated was drastic.

She had been thinking of a way to make a lot of money—fast and tax-free.

One of the loved ones asked her if she was going to sell her body.

She replied, "In a manner of speaking—yes. Yes, I am."

That was the end. The motive was there. Part of the plan was there.

All they had to do was wait until the transaction was complete, like spiders in a web.

That's what they did.

The wait had ended moments ago, after the strong one strangled the girl to death. Now, they were on to the next step—hiding the body.